. . . Jan opened the door wide and held her breath because Victoria was so beautiful and because she was really there. She took one of Victoria's cold hands and drew her inside and closed the door and locked it.

Victoria said, Oh, Jan, and Jan put her arms around her in under the wrap and held her close and kissed her for the first time without gentleness, without caution. When Victoria opened her eyes she said, I love you with my whole heart, Jan. Please look happy about it, say something about it.

You're here, Jan said, and now I believe you're here.

WE TOO ARE DRIFTING

WE TOO ARE DRIFTING
a novel by
Gale Wilhelm

the NAIAD PRESS inc.
1984

Printed in the United States of America
First Naiad Press Edition 1984

Typeset by Sandi Stancil
Cover design by Tee A. Corinne

ISBN 0-930044-61-4

For

KENNETH HOUSTON

WORKS BY GALE WILHELM

WE TOO ARE DRIFTING   1935

NO LETTERS FOR THE DEAD   1936

TORCHLIGHT TO VALHALLA   1938*

BRING HOME THE BRIDE   1940

THE TIME BETWEEN   1942

NEVER LET ME GO   1945

*Available Fall, 1985 from Naiad Press

GALE WILHELM & HELEN HOPE RUDOLPH PAGE
1939

HELEN HOPE RUDOLPH PAGE
CA. 1941 or 1942
PHOTOGRAPHER GALE WILHELM

INTRODUCTION

Poor little leaves,
We too are drifting,
Someday it will be autumn.

From the yellowing pages of mid-thirties and forties magazines and newspapers, out of the single publicity photo which appeared as each of her six books was published, she looks levelly at the viewer. Jeannette H. Foster, before outlining the plot of this classic and luminous lesbian novel in *Sex Variant Women in Literature*, described her: "...a young woman pictured frankly on the dust jacket as shingled and tailored...."

We know just enough about Gale Wilhelm to be tantalized.

Born April 26, 1908, in Eugene, Oregon to Ethel Gale Brewer and Wilson Price Wilhelm, Gale Wilhelm was educated in Oregon, Idaho, and Washington. As a young adult she moved to the Bay area near San Francisco and Berkeley, and lived there for ten years.

Prior to 1935 we know that several sonnets appeared in *Overland Magazine.* And then came *We Too Are Drifting.*

In 1935 depression-torn America, homosexuality was far less acceptable a topic than it is now. Considering the times, it is a clear measure of Gale Wilhelm's talent that Random House chose to publish the book, and to promote it. And it is a clear validation of the power and compelling beauty of this book that it was favorably reviewed in dozens of major publications including the *New York Herald Tribune, The Nation, The New York World Telegram, The Daily Mirror, The Boston Transcript, The New Republic, Books, Current History,* etc. The queen of the review world, *Saturday Review of Literature,* praised it lavishly, and even reproduced the now-famous publicity photo.

When this novel first appeared, Gale Wilhelm was living in New York City; we know that she lived there for a year. In 1936, her second novel *No Letters for the Dead* was published, to generally good reviews.

In 1937 she returned to the west coast. She lived with Helen Hope Rudolph Page, whom she called by the nickname of Chico. The happiness of her life at this time seems reflected in her third novel, the final book she would devote entirely to lesbian themes, *Torchlight to Valhalla.* It will be reissued by Naiad Press in 1985, and is a joyous complement to *We Too Are Drifting.*

Ironically, we know a great deal more about Helen Page than we do about Gale Wilhelm, for reasons which are sadly familiar to those who attempt to track the history of their foremothers. Only those women with a tie to a significant male have been deemed worthy of recording. Helen Page, a great grandniece of Stephen A. Douglas, was associated with Carl Sandburg in his work on his famous four-volume biography of Abraham Lincoln. In the course of this research Carl Sandburg became a close friend of both women and visited them in Oakdale several times.

For approximately fifteen years Gale Wilhelm lived with Helen Page, along with Helen's mother as well, for a time. Helen ran the Oakdale branch of the *Stockton Record,* and much of the actual detail we know about Gale Wilhelm's life appeared in that paper's September 19, 1940 issue. Ostensibly a serious article about the author of a newly published fourth novel *Bring Home the Bride,* it is, in fact, a campy tongue-in-cheek portrait of a very butchy woman: ". . . She lives the discreetly boisterous life of a country gentlewoman . . . She also shoots craps and swings a wicked dice cup . . . Her clothes are simple past severity . . . (She) is expert at applying bloody nail polish—to the fingers of her friends—not her own." The article's tone is deliberately provocative: ". . . She knows, more than she knows any other thing, that things are not what they seem, that the conventional aspect of things can be the least true . . . And she has absorbed the great truth of modern psychology—that "normal" is an abstraction, that there is no such thing as a normal person."

In 1943 Gale Wilhelm published two stories, in *Colliers* and *The Yale Review.* In December, 1943, she was awarded an honorary membership in the International Mark Twain Society for "outstanding contribution in the field of fiction." Her last novel, *Never Let Me Go,* appeared in 1945, with a cover blurb by Carl Sandburg. As late as winter, 1945, Sandburg's letters indicate he was planning another visit to Oakdale. (Those interested, and with access to the University of Illinois–Urbana–Champaign, will find letters between the women and Carl Sandburg among his correspondence which is housed there.)

The tracks fade then, become fuzzy. We know that Gale and Helen lived in Oakdale until Helen's death in the mid-fifties—and that Helen did not deed the house over to Gale. As yet we do not know where Gail Wilhelm went after this. The last biographical note we have appears in 1951, in Harry Warfel's marvelous source book, *American Novelists of Today*. The photo of Gale Wilhelm in this book (she would have been 43 by then) shows a sadly different woman than the glorious, purposeful face in that other photograph at the age of 27. This face is sardonic, and marred by a single deep frown line; the eyes seem to glare in fury at the camera.

If Gale Wilhelm is alive, she will turn 77 in April, 1985. At this writing we are looking for her, or for proof of her death. We hope to have more information by the time *Torchlight to Valhalla* is released in 1985.

In 1951, when I was seventeen and first read *We Too Are Drifting*, it would have been easy to find her. If there is any regret to be felt about youth, it is that you do not realize that you can actually do anything you want to do.

I gratefully acknowledge the help of Eric Garber in compiling this information, and the Carl Sandburg Collection, the University of Illinois at Urbana; and I thank other sources who prefer not to be named.

Barbara Grier
October, 1984

WE TOO ARE DRIFTING

SHE thought I'll wait ten minutes more and rose and went swiftly to the window beyond the big stone Pearl Fisher. She walked swiftly and lightly, saying, Sorry. Not just now. Hello. Sorry. Hello Max. Not just now, thanks, and then she stood against the big tall window looking east into the dark spattered with lights and rain. She set her shoulders and her thoughts against the room, she stood very still by the window and thought, Surely it's not lost, there must be a place in me where it's hidden, surely I'll find it again. Behind her someone laughed like a ferryboat shouldering thick fog. That was Kletkin. She turned and looked toward the laugh, and she found Kletkin smiling at her through the smoke and voices. Whenever she looked at Kletkin she felt a warmth around her heart, his name was a hand warming it. She looked at him and asked, and still smiling he shook his head. He stood there talking and smiling at her over people's heads. Kletkin the eagle in a humming-bird's nest.

When she looked at her watch she found that she had waited exactly twelve minutes.

Kletkin joined her in the entry. He put his big hands in his trousers pockets and looked at her hands buckling her belt. When you buckle it that tight, he said smiling, I know you've got a fever.

She looked up at him. Why didn't you tell me it was going to be a mass-meeting?

Kletkin pulled at his frayed rope hair. Well, how the hell did I know?

19

Above the noise in the studio a girl laughed suddenly like a colt with fresh sunlight in its eyes and its feet electric. Jan turned up her collar. Well, she said, Meyer can't expect me to wait half an hour at a mass-meeting.

Kletkin turned and got a coat off the wall and struggled into it. It wasn't his coat and it wouldn't button. Come on then, he said. Meyer'll be sore.

And what then? Jan said.

Kletkin opened the door. Come on. I haven't got all night.

Outside they walked close together up the walk and up the steps and across the black pavement shining with rain. It was soft tender rain.

I like a night like this better than anything in the world, Jan said.

Kletkin shook his head. Oh no you don't.

And the thing I like least, Jan said, is a mass-meeting.

Listen, I asked three people, Kletkin said. Now is it my fault or not?

I like this better than anything in the world, Jan said.

I give up, Kletkin said.

They were descending the hill, walking close together, their feet slipping frequently on the wet pavement. The too-short unbuttoned coat left Kletkin's right side uncovered. His left arm was around Jan's shoulders. In the rain his hair was beginning to lift and curl. A little boy came up the hill whistling loudly against the dark and passed them without looking up. Kletkin tightened his arm around Jan's shoulders and said suddenly, If they get the kid up I'll crack somebody's head. You weren't there that night. Some harebrain pulled Sparrow's leg and she got the kid up and when I got there he was sitting on Saint Anthony's neck holding a bottle of port.

Jan smiled. You shouldn't have a Saint Anthony for him to sit on.

Yeah? Well, if they get him up I'll crack somebody's head.

They won't, Jan said, they're too busy telling each other what fine people they are.

They were off the hill now, they could take good long free steps. The rain came softly. Jan had lost the memory of the crowded room and there was only the cool gentle rain and Kletkin and the street deserted and a beautiful deep clean space for her mind. Don't come any farther, she said. If anybody asks tell them I got a headache and you helped me walk it home.

They stopped. Across the square the twin spires of the church lost their crosses in the night. In the square the trees slept in the rain, the grass slept under the trees.

Okay, Kletkin said, I'll tell them, but Meyer'll be sore.

He might have got there then, Jan said.

Kletkin smiled. Okay, fellow, I'll tell them I helped you walk a headache home.

They looked at each other and then she went on and Kletkin waited until she was across the street and then he turned back. He wedged his big hands into the pockets of the coat. The rain was fine on his face. He wondered when Jan was going to get hold of herself again.

MADELINE was lying on the rug. Jan looked at her and rubbed her cold hands together. How'd you get in?

Madeline smiled and said, Hello darling, I told Mrs. Keel I had an appointment with you and that apparently you forgot to put the key where you said you would.

Of course, Jan said, feeling weary. She hung her coat over a chair and carefully spread the damp skirts out

on the floor. She went into the dressing-room and took
off her clothes and put on pajamas. She slipped her cold
feet into alpargatas and went trailing the blue ties along
the floor to the rug. Madeline closed *Wilderness* and
turned, stretching and smiling. Jan warmed her hands and
looked at Madeline's arms stretching out away from the
firelight. She felt the warmth like fine wine in her hands.

Well, did you like Meyer, darling? Madeline put her
arms under Jan's arms and closed them around her. How'd
you get away so soon?

Jan put her warmed hands behind her on the rug
and leaned back on her arms. She looked at the fire and
said nothing.

Madeline sat up. What're you looking so black about,
darling? Wasn't Meyer nice?

Jan looked at Madeline's face, avoiding the eyes but
looking closely at the dark hair away from the high forehead and the fine straight nose and the lips. I didn't
see Meyer, she said. There was just a crowd getting tight,
talking capital a art and telling themselves what marvelous
things they do. It wasn't Kletkin's fault.

Madeline smiled. Kletkin could have both your hands
any day he asked, couldn't he, darling?

No, Jan said, looking at the fire again. She felt the
weariness and resentment sharply now, she felt cold and
separate in the warm firelight. She sat there leaning on
her arms and wishing it were all over and finished.

Aren't you glad I came? Madeline said. I almost wish
I'd gone with Pierre.

It doesn't matter in the least to me where we are,
Jan said, but I'd rather you weren't here. After a moment
she turned her head and looked at Madeline and there
were tears spilling out of her eyes and taking black from
her lashes in small rivers down over her cheeks. Jan looked
at the rivers and said, It goes on and on, and except for

the dirty satisfaction we manage to squeeze out of our bodies, it's nothing. I hate it. When're you going to understand how much I hate it? She watched Madeline getting ready to cry into her hands and she said slowly, If you knew how tired I am of nothing.

It began slowly at first. Muffled in Madeline's narrow hands. I have some pride, she said. I don't have to sit like a . . . I don't have to listen to you. If it's nothing, she said, lifting her face out of her hands, whose fault is it? I give everything I possess to make it what you want, I give my time, money, all my effort to help you and you talk about nothing. She meant very little of this but she went on striking at Jan's cold dark face with words. You're not human, she said, you're something carved out of wood, you sit there and you're wooden, you haven't a grain of feeling, there's no place in you for gratitude or tenderness or any of those things. You're not human. Her face had the black rivers and in the warmth they dried quickly and no new tears came. You, she said, my God, *you* talk about nothing!

Here, Jan said wearily. She took the hem of her pajamas jacket and wiped Madeline's eyes and carefully wiped away the black rivers. She put her arms around Madeline and drew her down and kissed her and held her with the kiss until she felt Madeline soften like wax and then she lifted her head and said, Fishwife. Anything's better than hearing you say things we don't believe. She looked at Madeline and smiled a little and said, It's a pity you were put together so nicely.

Am I put together nicely, darling?

Of course.

Couldn't you look a little pleased about it then?

I'm not pleased, Jan said, looking at her. I said it was a pity.

Madeline moistened her lips and turned her head

on Jan's arm and looked toward the fire. The fire had fallen into a small soft warmth of ashes. There was no sound; the rain made no sound, though the ceiling went up into the slope of the roof and when rain came violently Jan said it was just as if you were wearing the room for a sou'wester. Madeline listened and looked at the ashes glowing. She knew somewhere in Jan there was warmth and softness, she gave these things to Kletkin casually but to no one else. She moved her head on Jan's arm and said very gently, I'll find it someday darling, the key to you I mean, and then I'll unlock you and see . . .

Someday I'll kill you, Jan said. She lifted Madeline up. I'm going to bed. Try to remember this time your toothbrush is the red one.

MADELINE had gone when Jan woke. Sometimes, when it was time for Madeline to go, Jan pretended sleep, lying with her face in her arms and her breath even and undisturbed, and Madeline sat on the bed and looked at her, fearing and wanting to wake her, and fear winning. She kissed Jan's hair or tucked the covers up over her brown shoulder or she just sat there looking at her and Jan was slim and awake and quite still, and Madeline rose and went quietly out and down two flights of stairs and out into the street. But this morning Jan slept soundly, and when she woke Madeline's place was only faintly warm and she had left one of her little notes written on the back of her card and lying on the pillow. Darling please meet me at Ann's at four. It's important. I love you terribly. Jan folded the cardboard twice and aimed for the fireplace and threw. A little puff of ashes went up and settled slowly like snow falling. She got her cigarette case off the chair by the bed and lit a cigarette and lay on her side smoking. It was a fine morning. Sparrows fussed and gossiped under the eaves just above the open window. Good morning, Mrs. Puff, and how are the children this morning? Oh, good morning, Mrs. Paste, they're quite well, thank you, but Hubert is dropping his feathers at an alarming rate and I can't persuade him to eat. My dear, I went all the way down to Market street to pick up a few delicacies for him this morning but coax as I will he won't eat. Now isn't that too bad, Mrs. Puff? Oh, my dear, don't look now but that creature's up on the top insulator again. She isn't looking now. My soul, have you ever seen such brazenness? Jan lay on the bed smoking. The harbor sounds were pleasant, the street sounds were pleasant. She wanted to get up and get to work, but it was pleasant on the bed and she wanted to stay there more than she wanted to get up. Someone knocked loudly and Kletkin's voice muffled by the door said, Its Kletkin! and she said, What of it? and he came in. She put ashes in the tray and looked at him. He looked like a stevedore.

Good Lord, I'd hate to be so damned lazy, he said, going to the bed. He picked up the jacket of her pajamas and held it toward her. This yours?

Of course, she said, sitting up. She put on the jacket and buttoned two buttons. She ran her hands through her hair and picked up her cigarette.

This's special delivery, Kletkin said. Meyer wants you to do the pictures for a new book. He was sore as hell. Got any brandy? he said, looking around.

In the cupboard, Jan said. You ought to know.

Kletkin went to the cupboard and got the brandy and the siphon, a small glass and a tall one. He poured brandy into the small glass and put the bottle on the chair by the siphon. Jan poured a little brandy into the tall glass and filled it with soda-water. Kletkin said, Ah, and put the small glass on the chair. Jan drank down into the spray of tiny bubbles. She didn't say ah.

What I came for, Kletkin said, Meyer wants you to do the pictures for his book. He was sore but I told him you hadn't expected a crowd. I said you always folded up in a crowd and he said all right, but he wanted to see you and for me to arrange it.

I couldn't do anything for him, Jan said, looking over Kletkin's shoulder to the fussy sound of the sparrows. I read one of his books once. It was a big fat circus horse galloping round and round a ring and never getting anywhere and all those trappings and everything. I couldn't do anything for him. Tell him I caught the night boat for Madagascar.

Kletkin got a cigarette out of his shirt pocket and a big wooden match out of his trousers pocket. Listen, he said, talking smoke at her, you've got to cut this out and get hold of yourself. What the hell's the matter with you? She concentrated on the sparrows but he went on talking smoke at her. Lying in bed at ten o'clock! He looked around the room with his eyes getting brighter and bluer all the time. He saw the sandbag with a coat of dust over it on the table under the window. He grimaced and waved his hand at it. Look at that. My God, you'll forget how to hold your tools. Listen, you told me once, a long time ago, nothing on earth could ever get you down again. He looked at her and saw her eyes clear and intent in her dark face and he said, Here you are in bed at ten o'clock. For a nickel I'd make you over.

Try it, Jan said.

Kletkin laughed. The tranquility came back into his eyes. Careful, he said. That stuff may go sometimes, but don't forget I can tie you and anybody else into a close little bowknot any time I feel like it.

Of course, Jan said. And you can tear telephone books in two.

Kletkin slipped his left hand down inside his belt. Well, what about Meyer?

Meyer can go to hell, Jan said. Abruptly she gave up trying to eavesdrop on the sparrows. Tell him I caught the night boat to Martinique. I'm down there now absorbing lots of rum. Let's have another drink.

She poured them and Kletkin watched her hands and wished to God she'd get hold of herself again and cut out being a fool. She had fine hands with hard muscles over the bones and the bones small but not too small. He had always wanted to model her right hand holding a tool. Matter of fact, he said suddenly, I'd like to do you entirely. Oh Lord yes! He jumped up and rammed his other hand down under his belt. His eyes got bright and wild again. The cigarette bobbed up and down in the center of his mouth. Look, Jan! Hermaphroditus! You're lying on your belly looking down into the pool. This's before, see? You get it, Jan? He stared at Jan as if he were seeing her for the first time and said, You're long and narrow and just right to the soles of your feet. Why didn't I think of this years ago?

It's a pity you didn't, Jan said. Here.

Kletkin took the little glass and swallowed the brandy.

And it's a pity you have to throw good brandy around like that, Jan said. She had to get up. Her pajama trousers were somewhere in bed, she felt for them with her feet and found them at the foot of the bed.

Kletkin pulled at his rope hair. Look, Jan, in bronze it'll be . . .

You're an idiot, Jan said, pulling on her trousers.

Oh Lord, Kletkin said, getting quiet and serious, it's too wonderful to think about.

Of course, Jan said, save the brain. Now give me five minutes, will you? and she went barefooted through the dressing-room into the bathroom.

Kletkin sat on the bed and locked his big hands between his knees and thought about Jan in bronze. He knew he was going to do this thing and he knew it was going to be good. It was going to be better than Sleeping Boy, better than Saint Anthony, even better than the Pearl Fisher. He stood up. He was crazy to get at this thing. Old Bellows' head could wait. He walked to the table and wiped the dust off the sandbag and wiped his hand on the seat of his trousers.

Jan came in and sat on the bed and put on her alpargatas and tied the ties. Kletkin came over and stood in front of her. She straightened up and crossed her legs and smoothed the wrinkled white cloth along her thigh.

We'll start tomorrow, Kletkin said, tomorrow morning.

She looked up at him and smoothed the cloth down over her knee and held her hand there. She heard the sparrows and didn't want to.

Now what about Meyer? Kletkin said. Want me to tell him . . .

Tell him I caught the night boat for Havana, Jan said.

Okay, I'll tell him. And you come up tomorrow and come early.

I haven't said I'd come at all, Jan said.

You don't have to. Kletkin sat on the bed beside her. He clenched his fist and set it like a seal on the back of her hand. You're a good fellow and I want you to do this and you're going to do it, aren't you?

Of course, Jan said.

SHE said hello to Ann Carr and looked over her shoulder at Madeline and Madeline smiled and closed a big notebook and said, Just a moment, Jan. Jan nodded and turned her back to them and went to the window. There was fog in the sky clouding the sun and in the street there was movement and faint sound and it was all pleasant. She lit a cigarette and looked down into the street. A door closed and Madeline's swift light steps came and Madeline slipped her hand through Jan's arm and said, Darling, you look so marvelous I think I'm good for you. She held Jan's arm against her left breast and for a moment held her cheek against Jan's shoulder. Darling, I'm so terribly, terribly sorry I said all those things last night.

Of course, Jan said, looking down into the street. You told me.

Your jacket needs pressing, darling. And you had your hair trimmed, didn't you? Jan, I want you to come to my house for tea today. She felt Jan's arm move and she said quickly and very low, Oh, darling, just this once, couldn't you? Ann's bringing Tonia Salvati, you know, who's dancing here this week; she's charming and it won't bore you a bit.

Jan looked at her. Did I come down here just to tell you for the hundredth time I won't go to your house?

The door behind them opened and Madeline stood away from Jan slightly but kept her hand on her arm. Will you come if we stay downtown then?

Well, I *believe* I'm ready, Ann said. Do I look a rummage sale? Glory, what a day! She was small and smart and she had merry brown eyes like a squirrel's. We'll pick up Tonia first and then get Victoria.

Madeline moistened her lips. Ann, dear, would you mind very much staying downtown this afternoon? She was smiling and tight inside about it. Jan's got some damned arrangement with a lawyer, wasn't it a lawyer, Jan? and she can't possibly make it, unless . . .

Why, I shouldn't mind in the least, Ann said, touching Jan's eyes with her bright squirrel's eyes.

And it'll be all right with Tonia and Victoria? Madeline said.

Ann snapped her glove into her palm. Oh, absolutely. I'll ring Victoria and tell her we're staying downtown. Where do you want to go? But let's get out of here before John discovers I'm around.

JAN looked at Tonia Salvati and sipped brandy and soda and did nothing about Madeline's knee. The music was soft and everything in the room was subdued and pleasant and not exciting. Tonia looked at her frequently with the frankest sort of curiosity and Jan wasn't annoyed. She watched Tonia and rather enjoyed her. She moved her nostrils and her eyes and her really beautiful dancer's hands and talked almost without pause. Jan struck a match for Madeline's cigarette and looked at her and said in a low voice, And this amuses you. She saw the anxiety in Madeline's eyes almost before Madeline felt anxiety and she smiled to reassure her and said, It's all right.

The waiter came and behind him came a lovely young girl who looked at them with luminous dark eyes and a smile that said hello, I'm terribly sorry I'm late but it's marvelous to be here, a smile that was shyness and apology and sweetness. The waiter drew out her chair and she said, Hello.

Oh, Victoria! Ann said, turning. She took the girl's hand. Madeline, of course you remember Victoria.

Madeline smiled. Of course. How are you, Victoria?

Tonia, Ann said, Tonia Salvati, Victoria Connerly.

The girl said, How do you do, and Tonia smiled and bent her head as if she were taking a call.

And Jan Morale, Ann said, looking at Jan.

The girl looked quickly at Jan and said, Not Jan Mo, and then she smiled the utterly sweet smile and said, How do you do, and Jan nodded to her and swallowed a great weight that in that moment had got into her throat.

Do sit down, Madeline said, smiling at Victoria.

Victoria said, I'm sorry I was late. The waiter seated her and she told him she'd have tea and instantly three women gasped and Ann said, *Tea?* and laughed upward with two sidecars under her tongue. Victoria smiled and told the waiter Lapsang Souchong and nothing else. I'm really terribly devoted to tea, she said, pulling off her gloves. I'm the only person left who is, I expect.

Jan held her glass and wanted to crush it. She couldn't swallow the weight of excitement out of her throat. She kept her eyes on the glass and on her fingers circling it, but she saw Victoria and the radiance that walked with her and looked out of her eyes and spoke in her voice. She heard Ann saying, I know, my dear; I understand perfectly. And Victoria's low sweet voice with the light in it, But I really like it very much. I don't believe I'm honestly sorry about it. Perhaps it's selfish of me but I feel it's the best thing that could have happened to me. And Tonia's voice, But how *in*-t'resting. Jan stared at her glass and wanted to crush it. She pushed it out away from her hand suddenly with the tips of her fingers and glanced at her watch and turned to Madeline. I'm sorry but I must go, she said, rising. She felt the weight lying heavy and alive in her throat and she looked at these four faces looking up at her and she saw amusement and curiosity and anxiety and disappointment. It was Victoria who was disappointed. She sat quite still with this disappointment darkening her eyes and falling like a shadow on her lips. Jan's heart rose like a fountain. She got her cigarette case off the table and said a very low inclusive good-bye and walked quickly away and out into the corridor and across the lobby and then out into the street. When she was in the street she found that she was carrying the excitement in her jacket pocket now, locked tightly in her hand.

THERE was twilight in the room and Jan stood with her back to the window and looked curiously at this big shabby room that had hidden and sheltered her for five years. The kalsomine was peeling from the ceiling. There was no color, no brightness. The room got only early morning sunlight. The little alcove containing cupboards and a gas-plate and a small sink was open to the room. There were doors to the alcove but she never closed them. It was clean but not tidy. There was a towel draped over the water taps, a box of powdered soap and a small cream bottle and an egg carton stood on the drainboard. The bed was only a box-couch and it was unmade. There were portfolios of paints and sketches on top of the cupboard by the fireplace. It was all ugly and untidy. It was a gloomy place. It needed color and light. She knew she was going to do something about the room. She stood by the window and planned, trying this color against that. It was exciting.

She got her coat off the chair where it had hung all day. She went downstairs and knocked on Mrs. Keel's door and the door opened and there were onions and Mrs. Keel with a red face and a worried look. Oh good evening, Miss Morale.

Good evening, Mrs. Keel, Jan said. I wanted to speak to you about the room, but if you're busy I'll . . .

Oh, not a *tall,* Mrs. Keel said, smiling now and very cordial. Come right in. Supper's cooking itself. Jan went in and Mrs. Keel closed the door and there were onions and men's voices in the next room. Now what was it? Mrs. Keel said. Won't you sit down?

No, thanks, Jan said. She leaned her shoulders against the door. It's the ceiling, she said. It's peeling. It's beginning to look messy. If you'll come up in the morning I'll show you what I'd like done. Of course the woodwork will have to be painted too.

This was the first complaint Mrs. Keel had had from Jan and she had lived in the attic for five years. For the last two years she had paid quarterly and the second quarter was almost up for this year. Now isn't that funny? Mrs. Keel said. Just this morning I was telling the mister it was about time we did a little fixing up, I said you can't afford to let a place go to rack and ruin for want of a little fixing up.

Jan reached behind her for the doorknob. If you'll come up in the morning then, she said, I'll show you what I'd like done.

I'll be up first thing in the morning, Mrs. Keel said, and I'll be glad to do anything within reason of course.

It's not a great deal, Jan said, turning the knob. I'm sorry to have bothered you at dinnertime.

Oh, that's all right, Mrs. Keel said. It's like I was telling the mister, a good steady tenant is worth a whole lot these days.

Of course, Jan said. Good night, Mrs. Keel.

Good night, Miss Morale. Mrs. Keel hung plumply against the edge of the door. I'll be up first thing in the morning.

Thanks very much, Jan said. Good night.

SHE had a glass of sweet vermouth and a big plate of minestrone at Joe's. She walked around for a while and then she went into a theater and listened to harsh Italian dialogue for ten minutes. She kept her eyes closed and she was sure she sat there half an hour but it was only ten minutes by her watch. She went outside and tried to walk her restlessness into submission but it was no good. She went home. In the lower hall she smelled onions only faintly now and behind Mrs. Keel's door there was laughter and remote dance music. Under her door there was an envelope cut open at the ends to make a sheet of paper and there was small swift handwriting completely filling one side. Jan, I couldn't wait but I'm so sorry to have missed you. I wanted you to go with Ann and me to Tonia's last concert. You weren't nice this afternoon. Darling, why can't you tell me of the things that disturb you? I know something disturbed you terribly this afternoon. Did you like Tonia? She liked you. Little Victoria is wild about everything you've done and she thought all the time Jan Morale was a man. I didn't have time to tell you about tonight. Why did you go like that? Why do you have to be so ungracious? Oh, darling, you make it so hard for us and you could make it so easy and sweet and wonderful if you would. Ann is downstairs waiting. Why are you always so rude to Ann? I should think you at least could be civil to her and remember that she gave you your first chance to exhibit when you weren't known at all. Darling, I'm upset about this afternoon and so disappointed about tonight. If you come in before nine, won't you join us? Ann has a box and afterwards we'll get rid of her and go driving. I want so much to talk to you.

Madeline

Jan folded the sheet into an envelope again and sat on one end of the table swinging her foot and thinking about Victoria's small lovely young walking body following the waiter and her face smiling all around the table with shyness and anticipation. She was young, probably twenty years old and she walked like grass blowing and her eyes were dark and bright and her hair was fair. Jan had no clear image of her face, she had looked at her face only twice, once indifferently and then once again almost blindly. Then how had the excitement got into her throat? What in the voice, in the body walking had shown her that radiance? She didn't know. She had felt it, she knew it was there. Victoria. Her name was Victoria. Little Victoria is wild about everything you've done. She stood up and crumpled the envelope and held it a moment and then tossed it into the fireplace. She went to bed and lay still but her nerves were singing and vibrating like harp strings and she wanted to clench herself on something.

TALK if you want to, Kletkin said, but don't bob your head.

It's cold, Jan said.

I know, Kletkin said. There's no way to heat this damned barn. I can't very well stretch you out on the kitchen table, can I? Jan, remember that day it was so cold your breath showed and we went into the ocean down there this side of Pigeon Point?

Yes, Jan said.

I knew then, Kletkin said. The idea's been salted away in me ever since that day.

If you make a mess of it, Jan said, I'll come up here some night with a mallet and make powder out of it.

Kletkin shook his head. I won't make a mess of it. What'd you get your hair cut for?

I just thought of it, Jan said.

Well, from now on, don't, Kletkin said. Yesterday it was just right. Tired?

I'm too damned cold to be tired, Jan said.

Five more minutes, Kletkin said. He had never in his life felt so happy working.

A fly buzzed against the window. A tugboat tooted. In the kitchen Sparrow was singing without words.

Where's David?

Kletkin rubbed his nose with the upper side of his wrist. He's out somewhere. How do you keep yourself in shape, Jan? You don't do anything.

I drink lots of brandy, Jan said, smiling a little.

Kletkin smiled too and slapped a little wad of clay back onto the board. Okay, he said. He covered the figure. Now, he said, wiping his hands, we'll go for a walk to take the kinks out of you and you can tell me about this painting business.

Jan lifted herself slowly. *Walk?* she said. Good Lord, I can't even sit up. Give me a cigarette.

Kletkin lit a cigarette for her and handed her his robe.

I ache to the marrow, she said, sitting up and slipping her arms into the sleeves of the robe. She took the cigarette and stood up. The hem of the robe touched the floor all around her. She tied the cord tightly and said, This's like crawling inside a bear. Let's go into the kitchen and get behind the stove.

Okay. Better put your shoes and socks on. Kletkin was pleased and happy about everything. He unlocked the door and opened it. Sparrow, he said out the door, got a good fire?

Sparrow's voice said, Yes, come on in.

Jan didn't tie her shoe laces. She was terribly cold and tired. She went behind Kletkin into the kitchen. The tips on her shoe laces flicked out snapping at the floor as she walked. Sparrow was stirring something on the stove. She smiled over her shoulder and went on stirring. She had sharp brown little elbows and brown hair curling at her shoulders like a little girl's hair.

What is it? Jan said, going to the stove.

Beans, Sparrow said, smiling.

Kletkin laughed. Oh, that's wonderful! Beans again. He put his arm around Sparrow and hugged her and she put her chin down against his arm and smoothed the thick fair hair.

Jan thought they were beautiful together. And the beans were beautiful bubbling in tomatoes and onions and garlic and ground beef. She held her hands over the stove and nodded to the bean kettle. That's a beautiful mess, is it anywhere near being ready to eat?

No, not yet, Sparrow said. She put the lid on the kettle and Kletkin picked her up and backed to a chair with her and sat down. How did it go? she said.

Jan shook her head and looked at everything neat and in its own place in the kitchen.

Wonderful, Kletkin said, watching Jan. Like a top. She's wonderful. How do you feel, Jan?

Better, Jan said. She ran her hand through her hair and rubbed her warm fingers up and down her neck where the hair had been clipped.

Throw the cigarette away, Kletkin said, and you'll look like a monk in that thing. Sparrow, doesn't she look like a monk?

She ought to have one of those little caps, Sparrow said, smiling, and Kletkin laughed and held Sparrow closer and hooked his chin over her shoulder. Do you feel how perfect everything is this morning? he said to the bean kettle. How grand and perfect?

Sparrow nodded and Jan looked at them and thought how beautiful they were. It was good to see Sparrow and

Kletkin together and feel this beauty between them, it was a thing to believe in. She looked down at the robe and Kletkin looked at the bean kettle. He was pleased with everything. It was going to be a better thing than the Pearl Fisher. He looked up and his eyes stayed there looking at Jan's face. Her throat came strong and dark out of the robe and her face was narrow and dark and hollowed out under the cheek bones and the chin was strong. It was a strong face but it was blank as a mask. Her eyes were dark gray and you could look a long way into them, they had a marvelous depth and when she looked at you, you imagined she was seeing twice as much as anybody else ever did. She was thirty years old but she looked like a boy half that age until she looked at you. It was queer, you couldn't find a thing in her face but when she looked at you you knew her hard young boy's body was a lie.

Jan lifted one of the stove lids and dropped her cigarette into the fire. I'm going to dress, she said.

Oh, Jan, Kletkin said, putting Sparrow on her feet, what about that painting business?

Jan turned in the doorway. I'm having a cleanup week. They're doing the painting and kalsomining and you and I are going to do the décor. I'll show you.

Let's go now, Kletkin said. He lifted Sparrow off the floor six inches and kissed her. We'll be back at noon Pajarita and see if that, he nodded to the bean kettle, tastes as good as it smells. Get your clothes on, Jan.

OH, Miss Morale!

Jan turned and looked down the stairs. Yes?

Mrs. Keel waved an envelope. Mrs. Souchée said to be sure you got this tonight. She was here twice today. She said it was important.

Jan went back down the stairs. Thank you, she said, putting the letter in her pocket. Did they finish up?

All finished, Mrs. Keel said. She was dressed to go out, a little white paper plate on her hair, a white coat, white shoes and lots of rouge and perfume and earrings that couldn't possibly be as big as they seemed to be. There's a bit of cleaning up and they said they'd be up first thing in the morning and do it. I went up and looked around and I must say it looks nice and fresh. Oh, yes, I knew there was something else. There was quite a lot of mail and I put it in the cupboard by the fireplace. I thought you wouldn't want it lying around wi—

Thank you very much, Jan said. I'm going up to see how it looks.

Well, good night, Mrs. Keel said. I hope it's like what you wanted. Of course it's still kind of smelly from the paint.

Of course, Jan said. Good night, Mrs. Keel.

The room was large and white when she went in and it seemed strange and not her room. She opened two windows for cross ventilation and walked back and forth feeling the strangeness and newness of the room. It pleased her and it was exciting. The bed and the table were covered and there was a roll of canvas on the floor near the dressing-room door. She touched it with her foot and it felt alive. Tomorrow she and Klctkin would paint the doors to the alcove and the cupboard doors. She turned out the light and stood by the open window and looked out toward the water. The room seemed clean and pure. It was exciting. She didn't know why it was exciting but it was and this pleased her and the room pleased her. She thought of Madeline's letter and she put her hand in her pocket and she stood there looking out toward the water feeling the letter against her hand. The wind was cool and dark. Finally she took the letter out of her pocket and twisted it with both hands and threw it into the black mouth of the fireplace. It was a thick letter and it fell heavily. She went to the cupboard above the sink and got the brandy and poured a little into a water tumbler. She sipped the brandy slowly, standing in the strange new room with moonlight in the windows and cool dark wind. She felt very far away from what she wanted and knew she must have.

SHE heard the motor and knew it was Madeline's La Salle before the front bumper came abreast. Madeline drove a little beyond her and drew alongside the curb on the left side of the street. Jan went over to the curb and stood looking down at Madeline. She said, Hello, and felt nothing.

Jan, Madeline said, did that woman give you my letter?

She did, Jan said, smiling, but I didn't read it.

Madeline's knuckles showed sharply through her gloves. She moistened her lips. May I ask why?

Of course, Jan said. Whatever you may have said wasn't important to me. She stood looking down into Madeline's dark-blue eyes. Please, she said, whatever you do, don't start crying in broad daylight.

Oh, I'm not going to give you that satisfaction, Madeline said. I have *some* pride. Her hands loosened and clenched and beat gently on the wheel. She bent her head a little and her foot pressed the clutch-pedal half way down. Will you get in? she said, looking up. I'll drive you wherever you're going. But I suppose you're going to Kletkin's.

Jan nodded. It's too near to bother, she said.

Will you get in?

Of course, Jan said. She went around the car and

got in beside Madeline. She was carrying a package which she held carefully. I have some cookies for David, she said, nodding to the package. David belongs to Sparrow, Sparrow to Kletkin. That's the connection in case you've forgotten.

I've never, Madeline said very low, I've never in my whole life seen anyone so obtuse.

As David? Jan said. Or I? She held the package on her leg with her hand flattened on it. The sun was warm on the back of her hand.

If you had any reason, Madeline said in the low voice. If you had the slightest reason.

Jan took the box off her leg and opened the door but Madeline reached across her quickly and caught hold of her wrist. Oh, Jan. Jan, can't you see what you're doing? She put her hand on Jan's and held it tightly. Darling, will you go for a little drive? I have to talk to you.

Jan looked at her watch. It was eight-forty. I have to be at Kletkin's by nine-thirty at the latest, she said.

All right. Darling, please put the box down. Hold my hand just for a moment. Close. Jan, I tell you you can't go on doing these things. There's a limit to . . .

Suppose you tell me later, Jan said. We have lots of time.

Madeline backed down the hill and into Powell street and then she turned into Union, heading west. She handled her car beautifully. Jan, sitting sidewise on the seat with her left knee drawn up between them, looked at her and felt no resentment, no weariness. Madeline dressed so nicely and was so beautiful when she was driving. Jan wished they were strangers and that she were looking at this handsome woman for the first time and wondering about her, wondering idly who she was and about the things she might do to occupy herself. Madeline felt the look and reached her right hand to Jan. Jan took it and said, When did I say we had to be back?

I know, Madeline said. She was calmer now and she was wondering where to drive and how to talk without losing her calmness. She slowed and freed her hand and gave Jan her purse. Give me a cigarette, will you, darling? She wanted so much to be calm. Jan gave her a lighted cigarette and she said, Thanks, and drove slowly, smoking and trying to think of a place to drive. Did you like Tonia, darling?

No, Jan said.

Madeline put her cigarette in her left hand and reached her right to Jan. I'm glad, she said. Jan put Madeline's hand down on her knee and covered it with her hand. Jan, why can't you always be like this? Madeline said. Why do you have to treat me like a brush agent? Does it really make you happier to treat me like a brush agent? Does it make you happier to run away and not tell me where you're going and bribe that damned woman not to tell me?

Jan smiled and put her forefinger in under Madeline's cuff. Do nice people always tell their landladies where they're going?

You might have phoned, Madeline said. You might have written me a note. You know I hate going up to Kletkin's. Are they through doing your room?

You see, Jan said, moving her forefinger, Mrs. Keel *is* an obliging person, after all.

Oh, Jan, why can't you always be like this? You're so sweet when you're like you are now. Are you staying with Kletkin?

No, Jan said.

Madeline moistened her lips. Are they through with the room, darling?

I expect they've carried out the last brush and bucket by now, Jan said.

Madeline looked backward swiftly and slowed. She waited for a truck to pass and then she turned around in the middle of the block and started back.

Jan smiled at her and said, It's nine o'clock.

Madeline glanced at her. Don't you want me to look at your room?

Of course, Jan said, but you don't.

SHE walked behind Madeline up the stairs. On the second flight Madeline dropped back and took her hand and drew it up under her arm. Jan looked at her. It's changed, she said. You won't like it. It's like a hospital. She got her key out of her pocket and unlocked the door, smiling a little and wondering why she didn't resent Madeline this morning. They went in and Madeline said, Oh, it *is* changed! She looked up and all around saying, It's like a convent, darling, it's so changed and white and so different! She took off her hat and walked away from Jan, pulling off her gloves. It *is* changed, darling, and so bare. Could we have a drink?

Of course, Jan said. What'll you have? She knew Madeline wasn't impressed by the room.

Madeline sat on the bed. Anything, darling. I got up a long time ago.

Jan made two brandy and sodas and brought them and stood in front of Madeline.

Madeline said, Sit down, darling, and sipped from her glass like a bird drinking.

Jan drank slowly and put the empty glass on the floor. She sat on the bed and said, For five minutes.

Madeline put her glass on the floor and looked at Jan with her eyes bright and dark and her hand reaching out and fumbling at Jan's wrist. Jan caught her hand and held it, feeling the swift lightning pain and hating it

and hating Madeline because of it. Madeline lay back on
the bed with her eyes dark and bright. Now go, she said.
If you can go now I'll know it's nothing. And then in
another voice, Darling, wait, I'll do it.

KLETKIN rose when he saw her coming and went inside.
She went in after him and leaned into the kitchen, saying,
Sparrow, here're some cookies for David, and then went
on into the studio. Kletkin locked the door and she un-
dressed quickly. Kletkin looked at her once and said,
Good afternoon, tortoise. She stretched out without
looking at him and put the point of her chin on her hands
and put her left foot over her right ankle. She thought
if she could fall asleep all this weariness and shame and
fury would melt out of her body. In some other room
a clock with a bell voice spoke into the stillness and
said it was eleven o'clock. Kletkin said, I ought to give
you a nice long face and ears a foot long. A little later
he said, Listen, you're not going to dive or anything.
He looked at her face and looked closely and then his
voice softened and he said, Come on, fellow, let's relax.

EVERY few moments she lifted her head and looked
at her new clean blue and white room. She had got out
a fresh block and her tools were lying in a row and she
was sharpening the graver and every few moments she
stopped and looked at her room. She knew exactly what
she wanted to do. When she sat in the theater that night
she closed her eyes almost immediately and kept them
closed but somehow she knew the row of faces. They
were old friends. The little boy with his mouth open,
the fat man with his face wilted in sleep, the woman
with the small dark mouth and the drooping chins, the

lovers' faces, the old man's face draped with great white brows and a sweeping mustache, she knew all these dark Italian faces whitened with light and they were hers. She knew she could cut them into the block with lines sure as a crow's flight. She finished sharpening the graver. She knew the other tools were sharp but she tried them all on her nail. Now she was ready to begin. She looked at her room. She was ready to begin but she didn't begin. She lit a cigarette and got up and walked back and forth. She walked across her new white rug and turned and stood in the exact center of it. This was a little white island in a deep blue sea. She ground her teeth together with a light rhythmic pressure. She looked at her watch. Eight-five.

She knew suddenly she couldn't work. She went slowly into the dressing-room and got a topcoat off a hanger and felt in the pockets. She did this automatically, thinking of something else. She went back to the table carrying the coat. She put the block away in the cupboard. She took the picture of the faces out of her mind and put it in the cupboard with the block.

IN the telephone booth she looked at the ash of her cigarette for a moment and then she took some money out of her pocket and opened the telephone book. Presently she took a deep breath and put a nickel in the slot and said the number. She felt the muscles tightening in her face and blood there. The nickel was returned and she put a dime in the slot and presently she said, Hello? Is Miss Connerly there? . . . Can you tell me where I can reach her? . . . Thank you very much.

She walked out into the sunlight with her hands clenched in the pockets of her coat. She couldn't believe it had happened so simply. She stood in front of the drug store looking intently at a piece of tinfoil flattened on the pavement. She couldn't believe it had happened so simply. She laughed suddenly and took a deep reeling breath of the morning. On the corner she paid twenty-five cents for an *Examiner* and slipped the paper back under the brown hands of the old newswoman.

KLETKIN said, What's the matter with you this morning?

She kept looking at the roof of a warehouse down the hill. I'm one day nearer the happiest day of my life, she said.

Kletkin laughed. Oh, then you've decided to have a happy day?

Yes, she said. She looked at the roof. She looked up at the sky. She didn't know why she thought about Michael and the day she found the dime. She was in the bathroom washing her hands and squeezing fistfuls of creamy brown lather through her fingers. There was a tall gray cabinet above the washbowl. There was a gray marble slab around the bowl. When she turned to get the towel she saw the dime behind the water-closet and she heard Aunt Rebecca calling Michael to come and get the basket and get down to Blaum's as fast as his legs could take him. She picked up the dime and hung the towel on the hook. She met Michael in the hall. Aunt Rebecca was yelling in the kitchen. Shake your shirttail, will you, young man? Michael pulled a bit of his shirttail out and shook it at the kitchen door. And don't let the wind blow the list out of the basket, you hear? Michael nodded at the kitchen door. She went out with him and they went down the steps. She gave him the dime and told him to get anything he wanted. She was being punished for something that day and she

couldn't go beyond the steps. She sat down and waited
for Michael to get the groceries and the candy and come
back. She saw him swinging the basket against his thin
bare leg and getting farther away. Then she saw Hans, she
couldn't remember whether his name was Dietrich or
Dieterle but it was one or the other, she saw Hans cross-
ing the street and he walked along with Michael and
then they stopped and she saw Michael hold out his hand
and she saw Hans's hand shoot out like a snake striking.
She was half way down the block before she thought
what she'd get if she left the steps. Hans saw her and
grinned and she ran faster and he turned and began to
run but she jumped and got one of her arms around his
neck and they fell together, Hans underneath. The fall
jarred her teeth and she thought she'd cracked her elbow
but she had Hans's arm and she pulled it back and up
and pushed his fist up between his shoulderblades before
he lifted his head. He was grunting and trying to get his
breath. Her hair fell down all around her face and she
blew at it and said, Gimme the dime. His fist softened
and unclenched and she took the dime. You big fat Dutch
bastard, she cried. She gave his arm another push upward and he squealed and she got off him. His nose was
bloody and tears were running down over his face. She
said, Get the hell outa here, and he got. Michael was
standing there and he looked at her and said, Gee! She
couldn't remember exactly what happened then but
she went into Blaum's with Michael and they got the
groceries and Blaum put the candy in two little striped
bags for them. They must have sat on the steps a long
time, talking about Hans and eating the candy. Michael
told her he showed Hans the dime and said Jan found
it and then Hans grabbed it and said he'd tell their aunt
they swiped it off him if Michael didn't divvy. They sat
on the steps, talking and eating the candy. It was candy

that stuck their jaws together. They made terrible faces over it and laughed a lot. A bakerboy passed with his big basket and they smelled the fresh bread and Michael took a big breath of it and rolled his eyes and held his middle. Across the street the littlest Schmitt boy decided to make water through a knothole in the cellar door and his mother leaned out of the window just above him and yelled loud enough to wake Frederick the Great, and Albert jumped and Michael got choked laughing. And then they saw Aunt Rebecca coming down the street wearing her bulldog face and they jumped together like one jack-in-the-box. They thought they were in for it but just as they got to their steps the ambulance came roaring down the street and backed up to their steps and their father came out feet first. So nothing happened to them that night. She saw all this in the sky and it ended suddenly and she said, Kletkin, Michael *was* soft.

Kletkin stared at her. He hadn't heard her say Michael for five years. I know it, he said, but . . .

You used to try to make me see it, Jan said, but I never could, could I?

Well, Kletkin said, twins're twins even if one is hard and the other soft as this. He waved a little wad of clay at her.

I always fought his battles for him, she said. It was all right when we were little but when he got big enough to carry me around on one arm it was different.

Kletkin looked at her. This was a funny business. She told him once if he ever said Michael to her again she'd forget she ever knew anyone named Kletkin. He looked at her and said cautiously, Ever see that girl?

No, Jan said.

Kletkin worked swiftly and easily. Yes, he said, Mike was soft. Born soft. You could make a big circus tent out of all the skirts he hid himself behind.

Jan wished she hadn't thought about Michael. She looked steadily at the roof. I'm going to rest a while, she said.

Okay, Kletkin said. He looked at her and wondered what had made her speak of Michael.

She stretched her arms down along her sides and turned her head away from Kletkin and closed her eyes. Two minutes passed very quickly. She took the position again.

Kletkin said, You eating regularly these days?

Of course.

Well, he said, you're five pounds lighter. It shows around your ribs.

Jan smiled and instantly Kletkin froze and got that expression and made it fast in his mind.

SHE was selling a bit of ruby glass to a very big woman who used a lorgnette. She seemed older somehow, she was serious and eager but not too eager and her face in profile was lovelier than anything Jan had ever seen. Her hair had the brightness but it was darker than Jan remembered. She was not tall not short, she held herself well and was small-breasted and small-hipped. A woman's voice asked Jan if she could help her and Jan without moving said, Thank you, I'm waiting for Miss Connerly. It was a long exciting business but finally it was over and the big woman swayed past Jan with a neat little package under her arm and Jan with tight muscles went among the tables toward Victoria and when she was beside her she said, Hello.

Victoria turned her head smiling and then the smile hung a moment and color came as if a faint rose light had passed across her face. Why, how do you do.

The sound of her voice was the sound of music Jan

remembered and she looked at her and said, Please have tea with me this afternoon.

I should love to, Victoria said simply.

The tight muscles relaxed in Jan's face and she smiled. You're through here at five?

Five, yes.

Where shall we go? Jan said.

Anywhere.

A little place, Jan said, or a big place?

You say.

Do you know the Green Gate? Victoria nodded and Jan said, I'll be there at five, and smiled and turned away. Walking toward the street door of the shop she felt wild and drunk. She wondered why she didn't walk into tables and upset thousands of dollars worth of china and glass.

VICTORIA said, Well, I met you first about two years ago. A friend of mine rushed up the library steps one morning and said Vic I've got a Jan Morale! We went into the library and she showed me. It was Night Bather. I think I've seen all your shows and I've always been terribly thrilled but that morning and Night Bather, she smiled and shrugged her shoulders, that's something apart.

Do they call you Vic? Jan said, watching her face. Your friends, I mean.

They did, some of them, at school, Victoria said.

Jan lit another cigarette. She knew she could never say Vic.

The next time I met you, Victoria said, was in Penny-weights.

Jan smiled. Woodcuts by Jan Morale. That's like costumes by somebody in small print in your program. But tell me, what was Victoria Connerly doing all this time? Was she a very serious art student walking up into

the hills every afternoon with all her gear to paint euca-
lyptus trees? Or did she like tennis and dancing and
football games and whatever else it is you do over there
in Berkeley?

Victoria laughed. Oh, but you see I'm not going to
school now. For all I know there may be an entirely new
set of diversions now.

Jan shook her head. I'm sure there's still dancing
and football games and tennis. And art students.

Victoria nodded. Her left hand lay relaxed and lovely
with a pale jade ring and coral fingernails on the table.
I'm convinced now that it wasn't the right thing for me,
she said, looking at her hand and turning the ring with
her thumb. Painting, I mean. If it were a necessary thing,
an inevitable thing, I shouldn't be able to put it aside
without any special regret, do you think? I mean I should
be wanting tremendously to paint all the time, don't
you think?

Jan put her cigarette out. Perhaps, she said.

I love pictures, Victoria said earnestly. I'm terribly
thrilled by them if they're good. Any work of art that's
really good moves me terribly and, well, it fills me with
fresh proof of my own inadequacy. I'm sure now it wasn't
the right thing for me. Painting, I mean.

Jan lit another cigarette. And what you're doing now,
she said, is it the right thing?

Victoria looked up. Her eyes were warm dark brown
and widely spaced. I like it very much, she said. You see
I'm with lovely things all day and that means a great
deal, don't you think? And I have a chance to go up. I
might even have a shop of my own someday.

I think, Jan said, watching her face, the something
of one's own is the most important thing of all.

Victoria looked into her cup and turned it and then
looked up with the thought in her eyes. Do you?

Of course, Jan said.

Then I shall have a shop of my own someday, Victoria said, smiling, and of course I shall have a few good pictures, a few good prints.

Jan smiled. And woodcuts by Jan Morale.

Oh, yes, Victoria said. The faint rose light went across her face. It's awfully funny now, but I thought all the time you were a man. Marky, that's my friend who has dozens of your prints, Marky did too. I mean we took it for granted that you were. They don't seem the sort of thing a woman would do somehow and, well, we simply took it for granted.

Of course, Jan said. People almost always do. My name's Janice but I haven't used it for so long it doesn't seem to belong to me at all.

Jan suits you, Victoria said.

Jan put out her cigarette. Just as Vic doesn't suit you.

Victoria laughed and took up her gloves and began to put them on. That's what my mother says. This has been so nice and I hate to go, but I must really. I didn't telephone mother and she'll be wondering about me.

Jan looked at her watch. If we're lucky about a taxi you can just make the six o'clock boat.

Oh, heavens, Victoria smiled and shook her head, if I took a cab every time I almost missed a boat I'm afraid I should have to stop commuting altogether.

Jan picked up her cigarette case and slipped it into her pocket. Of course, she said, but if someone you knew offered you a lift you'd take it wouldn't you? Well, I'm going your way and I'm offering you a lift.

But, Victoria said.

We'll have to hurry, Jan said, smiling. So far as I know they never wait for people.

HER hands were sure and strong under the light and her mind was sure but her thoughts kept turning back and away from her work. She worked slowly and steadily this way and somewhere out in the night a clock struck but she didn't count with it and somewhere out in the night an automobile horn sounded and a boat whistled in its throat and the horn sounded again, trumpeting out into the night, and Jan thought of all the people out there who didn't know Victoria and were poor. Her hands and her mind had a beautiful miraculous knowledge of what she wanted done. Out in the dark a boat whistled from the center of its heart and said Victoria and somewhere there were quick running steps and someone knocking on a door somewhere, someone with anxious knuckles was knocking and knocking. Jan frowned and lifted the point of the scorper carefully and said, Yes? and suddenly her hands and arms and shoulders fell apart with weariness.

The doorknob turned and turned and Madeline's voice said, It's locked!

Jan pushed the block up out of the circle of light and went to the door and unlocked it. Madeline was leaning against the frame of the door and breathing rapidly from the stairs and she looked up with bright eyes and a slow smile. Hello, darling, she said, could a lady use your telephone? She was quite drunk and very beautiful. Jan stood looking at her and rubbing the heel of her right hand. Were you asleep, darling? Madeline said. No, you never sleep in a smock, do you? I simply blew the damned horn off. Could a lady have a drink?

Come in, Jan said. I'll see what I can do.

She went across to the alcove and opened the doors that looked like great blue tiles now. She got the brandy and got a brandy glass and polished it. Madeline closed the door and locked it and put the key down the neck of her dress. Jan filled the glass and brought it, saying, Here you are, and put it into Madeline's cold fingers.

But, darling, aren't you going to . . . darling, you know I hate to drink alone. Madeline slipped her left arm out of her jacket and put her hand on Jan's shoulder. Jan, darling, what's happened? Don't look so damned black about it, darling.

Jan took the glass out of her fingers and slipped the sleeve off her right arm and put the jacket on the table. She put the glass in Madeline's fingers again and said, It's a very nice dress. I like the sleeves.

Madeline looked at her bare left arm. Oh, darling. She began to laugh. Jan put her hand up and steadied the tipping glass in Madeline's hand. Oh, darling, Madeline said, laughing, it's so silly.

Drink it, Jan said.

Madeline looked at the glass and kicked slowly sidewise at her long skirt. I heard a toast tonight, I heard the most marvelous toast for you. She stepped close to Jan and put her arm around her neck and said, The most marvelous toast about . . . She closed her eyes and bent her head and lifted it and said, Kiss me, darling.

Jan kissed her and said, Now drink it or put it down.

Madeline said, Oh, not that way, darling, and laughed and looked at Jan and at the glass with Jan's hand holding it steady. All right, darling. She lifted the glass with Jan's hand lifting her hand and the glass and she drank it and said, That was marvelous. You always have the most marvelous brandy. It was brandy, wasn't it, darling? It wasn't poison?

Jan took the glass out of her hand and put it on the table and Madeline put her arm around Jan's neck and locked her hands. Jan looked at her and looked curiously at her eyes with blue shadows and her mouth carefully red and she wondered how this Madeline was different and why she felt no resentment.

Did you mean it the other day, Madeline said, about never wanting me here again?

Yes, Jan said.

Well, I'm here, Madeline said, smiling. You didn't mean it.

Jan smiled and looked at her eyes with the blue shadows. I did mean it though.

Madeline slid her slipper between Jan's sandals and tightened her arms. You didn't mean it because you've said it before and you didn't mean it. When you really mean a thing you absolutely won't do it. When you said that time you wouldn't ever come to my house you meant it because you've never come. So you didn't mean it, did you?

Yes, Jan said.

Madeline said, You don't know what I had to do to come here tonight, darling. Pierre's somewhere having a fit. You haven't the faintest idea what I had to do, darling. She held herself close to Jan and held her face to Jan's face for a moment. Shouldn't we have another drink, darling?

If you like.

Madeline leaned back and looked at Jan. Darling, what's happened? Why don't you tell me what's happened?

Jan smiled and reached up to Madeline's hands. Unlock, she said.

Madeline unlocked and kicked slowly at her skirt and leaned against the table. Oh, darling, she said, you've got a new rug.

Yes, Jan said, pouring the brandy. Like it?

It's lovely, darling. Shall we sit on it?

Jan came with the brandy. All right, she said. Is your car locked?

Madeline nodded and then looked at her hands and moistened her lips and looked on the table. But I had my bag. I put it somewhere and I put the keys in it, I remember distinctly. Darling, where'd I put the damned bag?

Jan put the little glass on the table and held out her hand. I'll go down and look in the car, she said.

Madeline looked at Jan's hand and said nothing.

Jan smiled. You're in a bad spot. If you don't give me my key I can't get yours and if I don't someone else may and that would be a nuisance.

Madeline looked up and smiled slowly and said nothing.

Jan got the key from between Madeline's warm high breasts and went to the door and unlocked it and went out. Madeline moistened her lips and picked up the little glass and looked at it and then drank the brandy. She went slowly to the rug and knelt slowly, staring at the fire. There was something wrong and different and she couldn't find it. She moved her feet aside and sat on the rug, staring at the fire and trying to find the wrong and different thing.

Your star's out bright tonight, Jan said, coming in. It was on the seat and the street lamp making it much bigger than life. She put the bag on the table with Madeline's jacket. Now, before I sit down, do you want another drink?

Bring the bottle, Madeline said, staring at the fire.

Jan turned out the light on the table and got a fresh box of cigarettes out of the drawer and got the brandy and Madeline's glass. Madeline was staring at the fire. Jan, she said, something's different and I can't find it.

Jan lit a cigarette for her and she took it and held

it in her hand and watched its smoke. Jan lit another cigarette and sat down and stretched her legs out toward the fire and crossed her bare ankles. Don't worry about it, she said.

Madeline threw the cigarette into the fire. All right, I won't think about it, it's different and I can't find it. She put her head down on Jan's legs and was dizzy for a moment looking at the ceiling and then she was all right and Jan smiled at her and she said, I love you more than all the rest, darling, because you look at me that way, and it's different and lost and you never give an inch, do you? I mean when you looked at me that time at Ann's I was in love with you, but I didn't know it, did I? I didn't know but it was fun wondering how it would be different with you, and that night when I got frightened and you held me on the bed and then I wasn't frightened, darling, and in the morning you were sorry, weren't you? But I wasn't, darling. Isn't it silly?

Of course, Jan said, looking at her looking at the ceiling.

It's really so silly, Madeline said, because I love you more than anything else and you don't believe it and you treat me so badly. You know you treat me badly, don't you, darling? She reached for Jan's hand and knocked the coal off her cigarette. Jan said, Wait, and brushed the coal off the rug and put it out with the brandy bottle. Madeline said, Sorry, darling, and turned her head and looked at Jan and said, Darling, you've never said it and I want you to.

Jan looked at her. I can't say it because I don't.

But you could say it, darling.

Jan shook her head. It was four o'clock. She thought one more would be enough. She uncorked the bottle and filled the glass and Madeline saw it and lifted her hand. Jan held her up and held the glass and she drank the brandy and let her head fall back. Her hair was loosened and her eyes were vague and the blue lids sank and lifted and she said, It's all so silly, darling; let's go to sleep, shall we?

Jan said, Wait, I'll get you a pillow, and she lifted Madeline's head gently off her legs. When she came back with the pillow, Madeline's eyes were closed. Jan lifted her head and put the pillow under and Madeline with dreams in her voice said, It's all so silly, isn't it? and fumbled her hand up to Jan. Put your arms around me, darling.

Jan lay beside her and put her arm around her and said gently, It's not really silly, Madeline. You're sleepy and warm now and it's nice to sleep on a rug. She watched Madeline's face and said, Isn't it? It's so nice to sleep on a rug, isn't it, Madeline? And you're warm and asleep, aren't you? Aren't you, Madeline?

She was.

Jan waited a moment longer and then rose quietly and got a blanket off the bed and covered her. She turned out the light in the lantern and went to the table and turned on the light there and pulled the block into its circle. She leaned on the table looking at the block.

When she was working again she knew it was in her like a river under earth, nothing could reach deeply enough to touch it now, it was there in her like a river singing and running under earth to some sea.

AFTER the sun came up she let the fire go out and she worked on for half an hour with the room growing bright and Madeline asleep on the floor like a dead woman. Finally she put away the block and her tools and brushed off the table. She bathed and dressed and then lay on the bed for ten minutes looking at Madeline's hair, loose and dark on the white pillow. She wished she could close her eyes and have it all over and finished without any trouble. At eight o'clock she made coffee and she got a tall glass and cut a lemon and squeezed half its juice into the glass and poured in a little brandy. She took the glass and the siphon and went to Madeline and knelt and took her hand and began to rub her wrist gently. Madeline, she said, Madeline, I've got a drink for a lady. Madeline turned her head and opened her eyes and stretched flat on her back and lay staring. Jan smiled at her and they said nothing in that moment and neither moved. They heard the small rapid ticking of Jan's watch and they looked at each other and Jan said gently, Madeline, don't you feel it? We're on two worlds and they're so far apart. Don't you see it now, Madeline?

Madeline didn't move. Her face was still and molded with the immobility of sleep. Her mouth was pale, her eyes were very dark under the dark lids.

Jan said gently, If you only could see that we're on two worlds, Madeline, yours there, mine here.

What are you saying? Madeline said.

The same thing, Jan said, but I'm trying to be nice about it.

You are nice, Madeline said, you're nicer than anyone in the world. The coffee smells heavenly. If I could have a drink first to sort of put things where they belong, darling.

It's waiting, Jan said. When you're ready I'll shoot it.

I'm ready, Madeline said. She took a deep breath and sat up and said, My God.

Jan smiled and filled the glass with sodawater and said, All right, drink it quickly.

Madeline held the glass in both hands and drained it. Jan took the glass and they looked at each other and Madeline smiled. That's much better, Jan said. How do you feel?

Like one of those villages you see in the news pictures after a tornado or tidal wave or something. She felt over her hair.

It's all there, Jan said, smiling.

I can't imagine what I must look like, Madeline said, feeling her hair. I can't imagine why I was so silly. I didn't mean to get tight, darling, I mean I tried and tried to get away, we were at Ann's and everybody was there and Pierre was a beast and I couldn't get away.

Of course, Jan said. What about coffee?

Madeline nodded, looking at her crumpled skirt. I can't imagine what I must look like.

Not at all badly, Jan said, for a lady who came staggering in at three.

If the bathroom's still the second door and I can make it, Madeline said, I think I should.

We'll see, Jan said, taking her hands and standing up. She drew Madeline up and smiled at her and said, There's nothing wrong with you. She went with her to the bathroom door and came back and picked up the pillow and the blanket and put them on the bed and put the siphon in the alcove. She lit a cigarette and poured a cup of coffee. She knew Madeline would be in the bathroom a long time. She walked around drinking her coffee and feeling tired but feeling a deep warm secret elation.

Madeline came out with a nicely made-up face and her hair fresh and damp around her face and ears. Jan poured her coffee and she said, Thanks, darling, and sipped it and looked at Jan, thinking that she looked separate but not tense, not ready to flare like a match. She looked separate and serene and that was the difference. I don't understand it all, she said, looking at Jan. I mean it's so silly somehow. She put her cup down. What I really mean, darling, is that I feel such a damned muddle and you look so serene it's maddening. Jan, let's go a long way down the beach and lie in the sun and talk about it.

Jan looked intently at the ash of her cigarette. She thought perhaps it would be better to do it that way and then she thought it wouldn't. She knew Madeline too well.

Please, darling, Madeline said. I won't be silly and it's been so long since we had a whole day together. I'll go home and change and we can take some lunch or stop at one of those places down there.

Jan looked at the ash of her cigarette. No, she said, it would be the last day and last days're a sad business.

What are you talking about? Madeline said.

It's over and dead, Jan said. Post-mortems're a sad business.

What are you talking about? Madeline said.

Jan felt the heavy weariness rising and waking and she shut herself against it and said, Madeline, I've never said I loved you.

Love's a word, Madeline said.

Jan looked at the ash of her cigarette. It's so much more than a word, Madeline, all the words in the world can't tell about it.

What are you saying? Madeline said.

I'm saying it's all over and dead, Jan said. Shall we give it a decent burial or just heave it into the ocean?

Madeline stared at her. She moistened her lips and looked away from Jan and suddenly she rose and got her jacket and bag off the table and without looking at Jan went with her crumpled skirt and her dark eyes toward the door. Jan rose swiftly and reached the door first. She took the jacket and held it, and Madeline put her hands back automatically and slipped into it. Jan opened the door and took Madeline's hand and drew it up under her arm and started down the stairs with her. Madeline said nothing. She watched the stairs moving up under her feet and her head was in such a muddle and she was afraid she was going to cry. Jan watched Madeline's face and she was sorry and closer to Madeline now than she had ever been. She opened the street door, holding Madeline's hand close under her arm. They went down the steps and she opened the car door and Madeline slid under the wheel and opened her bag and got out her keys. She felt dry and cold inside. She didn't look at Jan. Jan put her skirt inside and closed the door. She felt close to Madeline and tender toward her for the first time. She looked at her face in profile for a moment, wishing she could have said it more gently. She went back up the steps slowly. She heard Madeline start the motor and race it. She went in and closed the door quickly on the violent sound of the motor racing.

SHE worked all day like a machine working in its own small world and knowing nothing else and never thinking toward the source of its energy. Late in the afternoon she stopped and made coffee and drank two cups and smoked a cigarette. She thought she would rest for a little while before continuing. She lay down and stretched out and fell asleep instantly.

KLETKIN knocked and said, It's Kletkin. There was no answer, so he tried the door and it was unlocked. He looked in and saw Jan lying on the bed. He went in quietly and stood by the bed, looking at Jan and thinking she looked small and slight and very young lying on the bed.

He sat down on the edge of the bed, careful not to

sag it suddenly and wake her. Her face was turned away and her left hand was under her head. The right hand had pulled free and the palm lay upward and the fingers curved over it slightly. He touched her hair gently with his big hand. He knew she was very tired to sleep like that. He put his elbows on his knees and locked his hands loosely between them and looked at Jan across his arm. He found himself thinking about something he had killed and buried long ago, but it didn't bother him now. He let himself imagine how wonderful it would have been to have found her the way he did and cared for her and got her gradually to looking at life again with her eyes open, all this if she could have felt what he felt at first before he knew feeling like that was no good. He smiled a little and unlocked his hands and crossed his legs. He sat there on the edge of her bed looking down at his big hairy forearm lying across his thigh. But it was all right. It was a good thing to have to take things as they came. Jan lost to him that way and belonging to him in another way that was finer. And then Sparrow with hardly a shoe on her foot and David already under that faded old blue sweater and her eyes full of something you couldn't turn your back on. A little mother for him, a little wife, coming to be these things and making him glad he hadn't turned his back. It was good when things weren't already made for you when you got them. Working at things was all of life. He looked across his arm at Jan asleep and he smiled, his big lined face tender toward her and this wonderful way she was sleeping.

He rose and went over and looked at the cupboard doors. He was proud of them. He saw the block on the table and he took it up and went with it to the window and studied it for a long time. He pulled his hair with his left hand and wanted to shout. He went back to the table and put the block on the sandbag and he stood there looking down at it and looking at Jan asleep on the bed and he wanted to shout. He opened the cupboard and got a pencil and a piece of paper and leaned on the table and wrote, You're a wonderful fellow. I want the first print off this block and make it a good one. Herm. will be ready to cast this week and it's going to Chicago. Wait'll you hear. It's pretty wonderful. That's what I came to talk to you about but you're having an honest sleep and I can't wake you. You're going to Colorado with us next month. Be good and keep the harness on. I'm busy as hell. As soon as you can come up and I'll tell you all about everything. You're a wonderful fellow. He put the paper on the block and smiled at Jan asleep and went quietly out.

VICTORIA took a deep breath at the top of the stairs and said, That's a marvelous workout! and laughed a little and Jan smiled and unlocked the door and they went in and Victoria said, Oh, what a charming room! and stood still.

Unfortunately, Jan said, rooms can't return compliments.

Victoria glanced at her and smiled. No, really, I mean we always think of attics as being, well, rather dark grubby places, don't we? and this is so bright and immaculate and it really *is* charming.

It's just been renovated, Jan said. Under its skin it's merely a grubby attic. Cigarette?

Thank you. Victoria tapped the cigarette on the table and looked all around the room, with her dark eyes very curious about everything and glowing. Then she looked at Jan and said, It's a bother having always to hurry but may I see the prints now?

Of course, Jan said. She got three portfolios and put

them on the table. While you're looking at them I'm going down and beg, borrow or steal some tea from my landlady.

Oh, no, please don't, Victoria said, but she was really more interested in opening the portfolio than in forbidding Jan to beg, borrow or steal tea. She opened the portfolio and said, If Marky were here she'd have to be held bodily. She looked over her shoulder and laughed a little, finding herself alone in the room and then, feeling a reverence, she took up the first print.

When Jan came with the tea in a white cup she was leaning on the table with her chin in her hands and her face flushed with the rose light.

If I were used to doing it, Jan said, I suppose I'd have put the water to boil before I left.

Victoria lifted her head. Oh, they're so beautiful, she said, looking at Jan. She looked young and eager looking up. They're so strong and sure and beautiful.

Jan felt her face darkening and this was a sweetness and she went on into the alcove and put the water to boil. She burned her wrist on the gas flame and said, Damn, on a sliding breath and aloud she said, If you see anything that especially pleases you it's yours, of course. She heard Victoria laugh and she turned and went to her and stood beside her with her hands like two held birds in her pockets.

If I were to take what pleases me especially, Victoria said, I should simply put all three portfolios under my arm and run for it.

Jan looked at her face with the rose light and then she looked at the print in her hands and it was Washington Square and not a very good thing. You'd really run with that one? she said.

Oh, yes, Victoria said.

Jan said, Then I'll sign it for you, and she got a pencil

out of the drawer and took the print and wrote For Victoria on the lower margin.

Victoria with the rose light darker in her face said, Oh, thank you so much. She looked at her name written in Jan's slanting handwriting and said, It's so good of you and I'm terribly grateful but you mustn't think I . . .

I don't, Jan said, smiling. While I'm making the tea you decide which you want and I'll sign them.

Victoria looked startled and said, Oh, but really I . . .

And I'm going to take a print of Night Bather for you if you haven't one, Jan said. I'm sorry I haven't one for you now.

Oh, if you would, Victoria said, because Night Bather is something so much apart.

I'm afraid this isn't going to be tea at all, Jan said from the alcove. I've no teapot and no strainer.

Oh, I've made it in the cup, Victoria said. Try making it in the cup.

A teaspoonful to the cup?

Yes, Victoria said, or rather less, it depends on the tea.

Jan smiled and put rather less than a teaspoonful into each cup. She thought tea was a nuisance but it was fun making it for Victoria. She poured the water into the cups and watched the leaves uncurl like little live waking things. You took sugar but neither lemon nor milk, she said. She took the cup and the sugar bowl and put them on the table and moved a chair up for Victoria. I apologize for it, she said, but there it is. She sat on the edge of the table and watched Victoria put two lumps into her cup.

Sugar? Victoria said.

Jan shook her head and said, No thanks, and stirred

up the mess of leaves and watched it settle again. She tasted it and it wasn't good tea. She smiled at Victoria and put the cup down. It's even worse than it looks.

It's delicious, Victoria said.

Well, but you're devoted to tea, Jan said. Did you decide?

Victoria shook her head. Oh, I couldn't do that. With this one and if you're going to make a Night Bather for me I couldn't think of taking any more.

Jan didn't want to impose them on her but she thought she'd really like to have one or two more. She slipped the bottom portfolio out and opened it. She looked through until she found Upstairs in Clay Street, two old Chinese leaning over their tea bowls. This isn't good, she said, smiling, but it will be a souvenir. Victoria took it and smiled at it and smiled upward at Jan and Jan said, And this is good but certainly not a souvenir, and held it out to Victoria. It was Six Flowers. Victoria looked at it and forgot all the others. It was a grave in moonlight with a single bouquet lying under the little cross at the head of the mound. She stared at it for a long time, feeling the cold and stillness in it. It's so terribly *like* a grave, she said in a low voice, I mean it has that feeling, the moonlight and the stillness and the flowers. Just one person remembered to take flowers.

Jan closed the portfolio and lit a cigarette. Exactly, she said, looking at Victoria. It was my brother's grave and it was my bouquet because there was no one else to remember to put one there.

Oh, Victoria said quickly, almost whispering, I'm so sorry.

Jan looked at her. No, she said. My brother was hanged for doing something you wouldn't understand at all.

Victoria's heart rose like a wave. She stared at Jan's gray eyes, cold and bright in the dark face. She was suddenly frightened and she stared at Jan fascinated and frightened by the gray stranger's eyes in the dark face. She rose, holding Six Flowers in her hand. I, she said very low, I must go. I've stayed so much longer than I intended and I, I can't really thank you for the prints.

Jan slid off the edge of the table. She lifted Victoria's hand and took the print and put it on the table, saying, I'm sorry, Victoria, I shouldn't have told you like that, I suppose. She stood looking at Victoria's hand. Victoria with her heart like waves breaking looked at Jan's face. She was frightened and terribly confused. Jan let go her hand and went to the cupboard and got an envelope. She wrote For Victoria on the margin of Upstairs in Clay Street and put it and Washington Square into the envelope. She hesitated, wondering if Victoria wanted Six Flowers now, and Victoria looking at her said suddenly, Oh, please, yes! She never could understand why Six Flowers seemed in that moment so terribly necessary to her and why it seemed so necessary to show Jan that she wanted it.

Jan put it into the envelope without signing it and gave Victoria the envelope. I'll get you a taxi, she said. There's a telephone downstairs in the hall. She smiled suddenly and said, But look, Victoria. Victoria looked up and the room had got gradually dark and there were shadows over the brightness. You see, Jan said, it's really just a grubby attic.

Victoria smiled uncertainly and looked at Jan's face, darker in the shadows. Oh, no, it's not, she said earnestly, it's charming.

NOBODY'S seen it yet but Hergmeyer and when he looked at it, Kletkin hit the table softly with his big fist, Well, you'll be poor all your life because you didn't hear him.

He's funny enough, but when he gets excited, my God!

So we're going to Chicago, Jan said.

It is, Kletkin said. *We're* going to Colorado and ride wild horses. He turned his head toward the door and said, Sparrow, bring us some beer, will you?

Sparrow's voice said, All right, in a minute.

I don't want any beer, Jan said.

Sure you do, Kletkin said, lighting a cigarette. You used to drink lots of beer.

Beer makes you fat, Jan said. And why don't you do your own bartending? Sparrow's got enough to do.

Kletkin looked at her. Why, she likes to do it, he said.

Jan went to the big window and looked out at the bright sky over Berkeley and it was miles away and Victoria was miles away under that bright sky doing some important and unknown thing. Kletkin, she said, I can't go to Colorado with you.

Sparrow came with light steps and two big glasses of beer. Kletkin looked at her. Sparrow, did you hear that? She says she can't go.

Jan turned around. Not that it wouldn't be fun riding wild horses, she said, smiling.

Sparrow looked at her and opened her mouth and Kletkin said, I've already told Karl you're coming and there'll be room for six your size and a whole lake at the front door and, well, why the hell can't you?

I can't, Jan said.

Kletkin took a big drink of beer. I want you to spell me driving. Sparrow couldn't drive Toothache in a million years and I'll get tired as hell.

I know, Jan said. I'd like to but I can't.

Kletkin sighed. Well, drink your beer. He drank and wiped his mouth and said, Got a commission or something?

No, Jan said.

Kletkin looked up at Sparrow. Can you beat it? he said.

Sparrow looked at Jan and Jan went to the table and picked up her glass.

Kletkin pulled gently at his hair and said, Can you beat it, Sparrow? but she said nothing and went toward the door, walking smoothly and quickly on her small light feet.

Thanks for the beer, Sparrow, Jan said.

You're welcome, Sparrow said. A moment later her high clear voice said, *Da*vie! Da*vid?*

Well, Kletkin said, it's a month off. Anything can happen. Once in a great while even a fool changes its mind.

If it has one, Jan said. This *is* good beer.

THEN if you won't, Jan said. I'll ride down with you on the streetcar.

No, let's walk then, Victoria said. We'll have time.

Jan said, All right, and they started walking side by side but not touching in the crowded street. May I carry the books? Jan said.

Oh, no, thanks, Victoria said. They're no trouble at all.

Jan took them. I want to see what you read. They were Burke's *Towards a Better Life* and Young's *The Medici.*

The Medici's for mother, Victoria said. I'm reading Burke.

Jan hadn't read it. She had read *The Medici* many times. She put the books under her arm. Walking with Victoria in the crowded street was wonderful. All these moving faces, the faces of strangers, thousands of strangers and none knew Victoria. Tell me, she said, what else do you do, what do you like doing?

Victoria glanced at her and smiled. Why, I don't know I like so many things.

Jan looked into the moving sea of faces. You like Viennese waltzes and Millay's poems and tea and dancing and reading in bed, don't you?

Oh, I do! Victoria said, laughing. How on earth did you know?

What else? Jan said.

I like window shopping, Victoria said, and Jan Morale's woodcuts and driving at night with the top back and bicycling.

Really? Jan looked at her. Will you go bicycling with me some time?

I should love to, Victoria said.

As soon as Sunday?

Victoria shook her head and said, I'm . . . and stopped. She didn't want to go to Sausalito with Dan and she hadn't really told him definitely she would. She said, Sunday will be lovely. See, we still have ten minutes, she said, looking up at the Ferry Building clock. Jan nodded and Victoria said, What about Sunday?

I'll meet you here, Jan said, and we'll go out to the shop I know and then we'll ride wherever you like, the Marina or the park or the beach or wherever you like.

Any place, Victoria said. Wherever you ride.

We'll decide Sunday, Jan said.

Let's go up over the viaduct, Victoria said.

Jan nodded and they turned left and went up the steps and walked slowly in the wind up over the viaduct. Half way across, Victoria stopped and leaned her arms on the parapet and looked down onto the tops of street-cars and at the crowds of people hurrying. The wind blew little wisps of her hair out across her face. She brushed at them absently and Jan watched her and thought that flying up off the viaduct would be a simple and wonderful thing.

This is the beginning of the nicest part of the day, Victoria said. She looked down the Embarcadero at the funnels of ships and the gulls and the fog thickening. Isn't it a pity all these people miss it? About Sunday. I'll take the eight o'clock train. Is that too early?

No, Jan said. Anticipation began to beat like a fist on her heart. She put Victoria's books on the parapet and got a cigarette and lit it, stooping over it and away from the wind.

I never can do that, Victoria said, smiling. The match always goes out first. She looked intently at Jan for a moment and Jan was looking down into the street and Victoria picked up her books. I must go now, she said. She wasn't looking at Jan now, she was looking up at the clock. It would be funny to stand here and miss the boat, wouldn't it?

Jan held her breath against the pain of the fist on her heart. I'll be at the flower stand, she said finally.

It will be lovely, Victoria said. Well, good-bye. It was good of you to walk down with me.

Jan said, Good-bye, Victoria, and stood with her back against the parapet and Victoria smiled and walked quickly away, with the beautiful ease, the swift beautiful rhythm like music. Jan stood with her back hard against the parapet and the music got farther away and fainter and then it was gone. She looked up and stood looking up and she felt the wind sharply now and she heard the thunder of wheels and feet and voices below her. That was another world. She dropped her cigarette and put her foot on it and walked slowly back along the viaduct.

THEY talked a little and pedaled steadily. The sun was bright and hot but there was wind off the sea and there was smooth bright green grass and dark clotted trees and the white sheep clotted and the blue sky and white wreaths and the smooth road curving. Victoria's hair was bright and loose on the wind. Her bare arms and legs were tawny. She wore a white sleeveless shirt and white shorts and dark sunglasses. Jan couldn't get used to Victoria with sunglasses. She was another person.

Tired? Jan said.

Oh, no, Victoria said, it's too lovely.

There should be a lake, Jan said. Yes, there it is. Shall we stop?

They pushed their bicycles up the incline and stood by the lake and the wind moved the water and moved a small white sail on the farther shore. Jan set the edges of her teeth together and breathed at it with her lips parted. Victoria was watching her and Jan turned her head and smiled at her and said, This morning has a wonderful taste.

Victoria nodded and looked out over the water. A day for looking at little sailboats, she said.

A day, Jan said, for feeding swans.

A day for watching the sheep feeding all in a close white flock, Victoria said, smiling.

All those things, Jan said, watching her face. She clenched her hands on the handlebars and lifted the front wheel of her bicycle slightly and it turned and the sun twinkled on its spokes. She watched the wheel turning.

Well, Victoria said.

Jan lowered the wheel and they turned and went down the slope and mounted again. They pedaled for a long time without speaking, but neither was aware of the silence.

WHEN I was very little, Victoria said, lying back in the chair, I was going to marry the boy who brought the paper every evening. I'm afraid he thought me an awful nuisance. I used to sit on the steps and wait for him. She smiled and looked out at the sky, lying back in the chair with the copper light full on her face and her tawny legs stretched out straight and close together and resting on her heels. I can't remember what I thought about it after that for a while. Then I was at Head's and I wanted to be a tennis champion because Helen Wills was. That was everything. Then I changed somehow and tennis bored me and when I went to college nothing was so important as painting. I thought I was in love two or three times but I wasn't and painting was the really important thing. Once Ann Carr showed some of my water-color sketches just to be nice to me, I'm afraid, because they were rather bad. But I painted and I read Russell and got horribly mixed up and unhappy. It was a phase, of course, because everything straightened itself out. You see, my father's bank failed last year and there were readjustments to be made, we moved into an apartment and sold things and at first it was terribly confusing for us, but it's all right now and dad and mother are quite happy. She stopped suddenly and the last word hung in the air like a lost note of music. She drew her legs up and crossed them. Well, she said, that's what I feel about it. If it sounded vague and, well, not very definite I suppose it's because I myself am. You're not like that at all, are you?

Jan smiled a little. When I was as young as you are I was.

Victoria looked up. You'll never talk about yourself, will you? I've noticed you turn things and slip by them or let them slip by you. She looked down at her hand, flattened on the blue linen arm of the chair. The light from the window was deeper on her face now. Jan, she said slowly, when you asked I knew why you asked. She folded her slender fingers under her hand and pressed them down on the arm of the chair. I think I knew the other night on the viaduct. Perhaps I've known all the time. She looked up and Jan was staring at her and she said, I wasn't surprised. It was something new and strange and rather lovely to think about. Otherwise I couldn't possibly talk to you this way about it, Jan. I've thought of nothing else since then. I wasn't really sure but today standing by the lake I was. Jan stared at her and she looked out at the sky again and said, It's such a strange thing and yet it doesn't frighten me at all, that's why I can talk about it this way. I never once dreamed of its happening to me and yet it's happened and I'm talking about it as if it happened every day.

Jan rose and stood with her temples singing and beating like wings in the dark and a darkness over her eyes. Victoria, she said. She stood looking down at Victoria and she said, Victoria, I want you to go now. I want you to think about what you've said and tomorrow, she took a deep breath and felt the darkness again, tommorrow, if you feel that it's what you should have said I want you to come. I want you to go now, but I don't want you to say good-bye, Victoria.

They looked at each other, with what they had said like a veil separating their eyes, and then Victoria rose and Jan stood quite still. Victoria looked at the cups and the glasses and the plate with one sandwich and the napkins crumpled on the little blue table. She looked at Jan standing motionless with her face dark, and she got her coat off the bed and went out. It seemed the strangest thing she had ever done.

SHE was still thinking about its strangeness when she got home. Dan was sitting with her mother on the sofa and when he saw her he came up off the cushion like a ball bounced and said, Hello Vic! She let him take her coat. She said, Hello mother, and got a cigarette off the mantel. Where's dad? she said, lighting the cigarette.

He went some place with Dr. Kerr this afternoon and hasn't come in yet, Mrs. Connerly said. Did you have a nice time, dear?

Dan came up behind Victoria and touched her bare arms lightly just above the elbows. She started and he laughed and said, Sunburn?

She looked at Jan's face in the fire and she wanted to look up at Dan but went on looking into the fire. She stayed there suspended and lost, trying to see through Jan's dark face, through the strangeness of her leaving the person alone to whom she had just said, I wasn't really sure but today, standing by the lake, I was. Why had she gone? Why hadn't she said, But I do know, Jan, I know as truly now as I shall know tomorrow.

Mrs. Connerly tucked her yarn and needles into the basket beside her and stood up. She leaned and kissed Victoria's cheek. Aren't you feeling well, dear? You look tired and flushed.

A little, Victoria said, looking at the fire.

You run in and take a nice hot shower, Mrs. Connerly said, and Dan and I will get supper. Didn't you have a nice time, dear?

She pulled herself down out of the lost floating sense of suspension and looked at Dan grinning at her with firelight along one side of his bony face and touching his brown hair with tiny gold fingers. She looked, attempting to smile at her mother. A bath would be perfect, she said. We rode miles and miles and I am rather tired.

Listen, Dan said, I felt a bad attack of backgammon

coming on this afternoon and I've been nursing it along for hours. After supper I'm going to take you for a . . .

Oh, backgammon, Victoria said, shuddering. Heavens, no! Not tonight, Dan. And, mother, I had tea so late I'm not in the least hungry.

Dan took her by the shoulders and walked her toward the door. Late tea, my eye, he said. Go wash the bicycle grease off your ankles. Wait'll you see our spread and then try saying you're not hungry.

Victoria got her coat off the chair by the door and went across the hall into her room. She went to the window and pushed it wide open and looked out into the sky to the glow of light over San Francisco. Jan was over there, standing alone in the high white room and waiting for that tomorrow.

JAN looked at her watch just as she picked up the graver. It was eight-ten. Just as she put the graver on the stone there was a knock on the door and she stiffened and the door opened behind her and Madeline said, Hello, darling. Working?

Jan put the graver with the other tools and turned. Hello, Madeline.

Madeline, dressed all in brown and wearing a veil, came and stood beside her. She put her purse on the table and began to pull off her gloves. Well, darling? Her hands became slim and white out of the brown gloves.

Jan rested her arms on the table and looked at Madeline with bright dark eyes behind the veil. Well? she said, smiling a little.

Madeline turned and leaned on the table and looked at the tools and the stone and then she looked at Jan and said, I was riding in the park this morning. Her voice was bright and dark like her eyes.

Jan looked at her. It was very nice in the park, she said.

Madeline picked up the spitzsticker and tapped the palm of her left hand with the flat of the handle. You didn't see me, she said, you were entirely too occupied.

Don't cut yourself, Jan said.

Madeline tapped her palm. It *was* Victoria, wasn't it?

Of course, Jan said.

Madeline moistened her lips. Victoria Connerly, she said, tasting the words. Little Victoria. Of all the people in the world. I suppose you know you couldn't have done a nastier thing, don't you? Jan looked at her and she looked at the handle of the spitzsticker and said, I knew you were unscrupulous and absolutely cold-blooded but I never dreamed you'd do a nasty thing like that. I suppose she's told you she's engaged to a nice boy who's studying law. Jan looked at her steadily and Madeline moistened her lips and said, But of course a little thing like that wouldn't matter an iota to you, would it? No, not an iota. She clenched her hand on the handle of the spitzsticker and said, I suppose you see it's all perfectly clear to me now?

I hope it is, Jan said.

You hope it is, Madeline said. Jan, why didn't you tell me at the first? It would have been so much fairer and better for everyone.

Of course, Jan said, but it happens that you're an unreasonable person and . . .

Oh, I'm unreasonable, am I? Madeline said. She began to laugh and stab at the table top with the spitzsticker and Jan said, Don't do that! and she reached out and Madeline jerked her hand and said, Don't you dare touch me, you, and somehow there was a long bleeding gash on the upper side of Jan's thumb and blood running toward her wrist. Jan said, Put it down, and Madeline stared at the gash and slowly unclenched her fingers on the shaft of the spitzsticker. Oh, Jan, Jan, I . . .

Jan moved her thumb. It was all right. There was no pain and nothing cut but the flesh, just a neat red cut and blood getting ready to drip on the table. She moved her thumb and the cut gaped and she said, Well, I'd better fix it up.

Oh, Jan, Madeline said, darling, is it cut badly, is it deep?

Jan rose and went to the bathroom. She held her hand under the cold water and got iodine out of the cabinet and pulled the stopper with her teeth. It was a nice long clean cut and not deep.

Madeline said, Oh, darling, I know what you think, and took the bottle and got gauze and adhesive tape out of the cabinet. She turned her veil up over her hat. Her hands were trembling and Jan smiled at them and Madeline said, Darling, is it deep? Should it be sewn up? Oh, darling, I'm so terribly sorry.

Of course, Jan said. Iodine is soothing, isn't it? Cool and soothing as hot iron.

Madeline was trying to keep the gauze tight and flat. Her hands were shaking. Her eyes were full of tears, the tears welling and thickening in her lashes. Jan said, I'll do this, Madeline. Cut a piece of tape, will you? She glanced up and smiled and said, Please stop crying, it wasn't my throat.

Oh, darling, Madeline said, I know what you think.

Jan held her left hand against her waistband and pulled the end of the gauze tight and fastened it with the tape. There, she said. She put the stopper in the bottle and put the bottle and the gauze and the tape in the cabinet. She washed a little spattered blood out of the washbowl and dried her hand.

You'll never believe I didn't mean to do it, Madeline said. I know what you think. She put her arms around Jan suddenly and said, Jan, tell me you don't think I . . .

No, Jan said, what I was thinking is something different. I was thinking it's a pity things always have to end with tears and the wrong words.

But I didn't mean those things, Madeline said.

Jan put her hands up and loosened Madeline's arms. I'm not going to look at you with your eyes spoiled. I'll bring you the purse and you fix them up while I'm getting you a drink. And then you've got to run along because I'm busy tonight.

Of course I will, darling, Madeline said, you know I wouldn't think of interrupting your work for anything in the world.

AT two o'clock Jan rose and stretched her arms and lit a cigarette. She left everything just as it was on the table and turned out the light. Little rivers of ice and fire were running outward from her heart. She walked slowly back and forth with the ghost of the amazing thing Victoria had said that afternoon. She went to bed and lay awake for a long time looking at the ghost in the dark groove of the ceiling. The cut on her hand throbbed. It was a second heart beating.

I CAN'T believe you came, Jan said. All day I've been telling myself I dreamed what you said.

But now, Victoria said, smiling.

Jan shook her head. Candlelight gives faces a dream brightness. I can't be sure.

Victoria laughed. She had drunk more wine than Jan

and more than she usually drank at dinner and it seemed very funny that Jan should doubt her reality. I don't know what I expected, she said, but it wasn't this, it was nothing like this. If you're really glad I came, why do you look at me as if I were, as if we were at a mourning feast?

Do I? Jan said.

Victoria nodded. When you opened the door you looked as if you were seeing a ghost and all the way down here you looked at me as if I were a ghost walking with you. And you ate almost nothing and you look at me as if I . . .

I can't believe you came, Jan said.

Victoria laughed. But I did and you watched me eat an enormous dinner and ghosts don't eat, at least not so enormously. She knew these things were stupid unimportant things neither Jan nor she herself cared about, but she went on saying them. Jan has anyone ever told you how splendid you look all in white? Jan felt her face darkening and tightening and Victoria said, You should wear nothing but white. You look so dark, and, Jan, I've been wondering how you hurt your hand.

One of the tools slipped, Jan said. It's nothing. She looked at Victoria's cup. It was empty. Her brandy glass was also empty. Jan signaled the waiter and said to Victoria, You don't mind, do you? The waiter came and Jan paid.

Mind? Victoria said. Not in the least. I'm quite finished. Jan stood beside her and she rose smiling with a flushed face and very bright eyes and said, Jan, if you could look a little happier about it . . .

I am happy, Jan said.

They went down the stairs slowly. Victoria thought there was one more step than there really was. Jan caught her arm and looked closely at her face. It's all right, Victoria said. She had never felt this way, never had rubber tubing for legs. Let's walk a little, she said. I'll be all right in a moment.

Jan held her arm and looked up toward the taxistand and signaled a driver. We'll have a ride, she said, and put down the windows and let the wind hold its hand on your forehead. She held Victoria's arm and smiled at her but she was bewildered. The cab drew up and Victoria got in. Drive out Marina Boulevard and back downtown, Jan said to the driver. She got in and sat in the other corner and let the window down. Victoria was small in her corner. Jan looked at her and looked away. Victoria, she said, I'm so sorry about it.

Victoria opened her eyes. The air's so cool. She took off her hat and looked at Jan. Poor Jan, she said.

Jan looked at her. She couldn't understand how this had happened.

I'm all right now, Victoria said. I shouldn't have taken the brandy, the room was so warm. It was all right till then. Don't feel badly about it, Jan. I'm really all right now.

Jan looked at her. You're so little and far away from me now, she said. Where have you gone?

Victoria sat up straighter and crossed her knees and looked at her hat. Already the restaurant and the candlelight and the enormous dinner and the long rocking stairs seemed another day. I spoiled it, she said, reaching her hand to Jan. She felt Jan's cool palm and her strong fingers with nerves quivering in them and she felt tenderness toward this hand and she felt a slow warmth like intoxication but sweeter. She drew Jan's hand up under her breast. Do you feel it, Jan? she said. I don't want to be far away.

Jan loosened her hand gently and took Victoria's head in her hands and looked at her and the light moved slowly across her face and then they were in the dark again and she said, You aren't far away, Victoria.

JAN tapped on the glass. The driver turned his head
and opened the partition a little. Jan said, Ferry Building,
Key side, and he nodded and closed the partition.

Victoria laced her fingers through Jan's. I don't want
to go, she said.

Jan looked at her. They were in Market street now
and Victoria's face was lovely in the light. I'll ride over
with you if you like, she said.

No, then I couldn't let you come back. She looked
quickly at Jan. Jan, come over and stay with me tonight.
Jan shook her head and Victoria said, But why? She sat
sidewise on the seat holding Jan's hand tightly. Jan, please
come.

Jan smiled at her and said, You're so little and sweet
and not wise. She felt the cab swing into the turn ap-
proaching the Ferry Building. There's your clock looking
at you, she said. Tell me good-bye.

THEY turned into Post street and walked up to Stockton
and crossed and walked back down the block on the other
side of Post, walking slowly and buying innumerable
things in the windows, beer glasses, a mandarin coat, an
etching, a jade necklace to match Victoria's ring, a black
dinner dress, half a dozen books, a hunting knife because
Jan was going to take Victoria's scalp some day and a
knife like that would be an excellent investment. But,
Jan, you have my scalp, Victoria said, laughing. Jan said,
Have I, Victoria? and they walked on. Finally they were
tired of the windows and they stopped and looked at
each other and Victoria shivered and in a small voice
said, When are you going to let me come?

They stood on the corner, looking across the street and feeling the loneliness of the street and the loneliness of the people hurrying. When you want to come, Jan said, you'll come.

But, Jan, I do, Victoria said. I've told you.

Jan watched a bit of newspaper hurrying along the gutter. What have you said about it to your mother? she said. She knew Victoria was devoted to her mother.

Why, I told her I was terribly fond of you, Victoria said. She asked me why I never brought you over home.

And you told her? Jan said.

What could I tell her? Victoria said. I couldn't say what you told me. After all, they do exist. Jan, won't you go over with me some time? Tonight, Jan?

Jan shook her head and looked at the fog sealing out the sky.

Jan, Victoria said, when are you going to let me come?

Jan turned her head and looked down at her for a moment. I? she said. God takes care of those things. She smiled a little and glanced up at the sky being sealed out. I think we'd better go, she said. Shall we ride or walk?

Victoria said, I don't understand you at all. Let's walk.

JAN opened the door, hoping she wouldn't see Madeline, and saw Victoria wearing a short red wrap and something long and white and beautiful. She looked frightened. Jan opened the door wide and held her breath because Victoria was so beautiful and because she was really there. She took one of Victoria's cold hands and drew her inside and closed the door and locked it.

Victoria said, Oh, Jan, and Jan put her arms around

her in under the wrap and held her close and kissed her for the first time without gentleness, without caution. When Victoria opened her eyes she said, I love you with my whole heart, Jan. Please look happy about it, say something about it.

You're here, Jan said, and now I believe you're here.

VICTORIA turned on her side and looked at Jan's watch. You shouldn't wear it in bed, she said, it's bad luck. She lay on her back again and put her hands under her head. Ten-thirty, she said. Dad's just backing the car out and mother's coming down the stairs wondering about her seams. As if they mattered. Mother's a darling. Victoria turned her head on her hands and smiled at Jan. Don't you ever get tired looking at me? Jan smiled and Victoria said, No one's really ever looked at me before. Jan, please tell me about you. Jan continued to smile and Victoria said, Please won't you, Jan? What you did when you were little and where you went to school and all those things?

Jan turned and lay looking up into the groove of the ceiling. There was no ghost now. Dear Victoria, she said. Two weeks ago today at ten-thirty I was eating fire and swords. What were you doing?

Victoria looked at Jan's face in clear dark profile against the white wall and her hair dark on the pillow. Had we fed the swans?

Yes, Jan said. You were looking at the windmill and you had just said, Oh I should love to live in a windmill tower, and then you said, Well, I suppose we *should* go. You lingered over the should and my heart almost broke.

Victoria turned and lay with her breasts flattened against Jan's ribs. Poor Jan, eating fire and swords, she said, smiling tenderness. She kissed the tip of Jan's chin. You're a lovely person, have I ever told you? And I love this room. I'd love to wake in it every morning. Jan, dear, please tell me about you.

Jan smiled and looked at Victoria's eyes and her lovely clear forehead and her mouth with the rouge gone. Dear Victoria, she said. How does it happen we were so long finding each other? You've been coming over here six days a week for a year now and I've been looking and looking, we should have found each other long ago.

Victoria smiled and ran her forefinger up along the part in Jan's hair. No, it happened this way, so this is best. But, Jan, think if Ann hadn't had us to tea that day. Or was it Madeline? Yes, it was Madeline because we were to have gone out to her lovely house and then something happened. How was it you saw only me and not Tonia Salvati and not Madeline?

I've known Madeline for a long time, Jan said, and at the first moment Tonia looked at me as if I were a museum piece and so there was only you.

Victoria laughed. And you ran away.

I ran away, Jan said.

Victoria put her head down. Jan, I did a terrible thing last night. Shall I tell you?

If you like, Jan said. She had known for a long time this was going to come.

Victoria lifted her head. Well, last night I was at the Mark with Dan and Marky and some more people and I was dancing with Dan and suddenly, whether it was the music or Dan I don't really know but I couldn't stand it, I had to come. I told Dan I wasn't feeling well and we went back to the table and I told him if he didn't mind too much I was going to leave. He said of course then we'd go home, but I knew he was having a marvelous time and I said I wouldn't hear of his leaving. I said I had a friend and I'd go up to her house and go to bed.

Which is what you did, Jan said.

The rose light came and went in Victoria's face and she smiled and said, Yes. She looked at Jan and kissed the tip of her chin and said, So I telephoned mother and told her I was coming here and Dan said he wouldn't let me go alone and I said certainly I would, so in the end he got a cab for me and I came. He was worried about it but he was sweet, he's really a terribly sweet person, Jan.

Of course, Jan said. All my gratitude to Dan.

I've known him for years and years, Victoria said. His mother and mother are terribly devoted.

Dear Victoria, Jan said, smiling and watching Victoria's face. You don't know how lovely you are.

Victoria put her head down. I want to be lovely for you, she said.

THEY stood on the wharf in the shrill crowded hour of activity before the boats went out. The gulls screamed and the fishermen chattered and eyed the women with their skirts flying like flags in the wind and people eyed the fishermen and everyone was satisfied. Jan leaned on the railing and looked down at old Gabriele. Would you like a couple of passengers this time, Gabriel'?

Gabriele looked up at Victoria's light slim ankles and her skirt blowing and he nodded, smiling, and said, Sure, sure. The little lady she gotta . . .

You're too eager, Jan said, laughing. How's the little one?

Rosa? Gabriele spread proud grandfather's hands. Oh Rosa she . . .

Yoohoo! Jan!

Jan and Victoria and Gabriele looked up, Gabriele with his brown hands measuring something in the air. Oh, it's Madeline, Victoria said, waving.

Madeline beckoned with a white glove. She was all in

white standing against the crowd. She was smiling and beckoning with a white glove.

Jan looked down into the boat. See you again Gabriel'. Tell Rosa hello for me.

Gabriele said, Sure, and dropped his hands.

Jan went along the wharf with Victoria toward Madeline. She wasn't happy about it. Victoria was smiling at Madeline and they were near now and she said, Hello.

Hello there, Madeline said. She smiled at Victoria and at Jan with her eyes bright. What are you doing down here with all the Sunday people? Isn't it a gorgeous day? I must warn you, Victoria, she said, smiling and bright in the sun, Jan has some disreputable friends.

Jan looked at her. I'm improving, she said. But don't include Gabriel'. He's a legitimate grandfather and a fine fellow.

Is he really? Madeline said. She moistened her lips. I was up by your house a few moments ago, Jan. Ann has some people and I was commissioned to pick you up. Incidentally I'm getting some lobsters. She held out the big package. The smelly things.

I don't mind them, Jan said, taking the package.

Thanks, Madeline said. Well, come along. Kent Southwick's there and lots of people.

Victoria looked at Jan. They started walking toward the street. Jan said, Would you like to go, Victoria?

I should love to, Victoria said, if you're sure it's quite all right with Ann.

Ann'll be delighted, Madeline said. Hergmeyer's there and Kletkin.

Jan looked up. Kletkin?

Madeline nodded. The car's down there. Yes, Kletkin. Hergmeyer brought him. Or maybe he brought Hergmeyer. Yes, that's more logical, isn't it? It seems he's done a perfectly thrilling thing of Hermaphroditus. No one's seen it but Hergmeyer and he's simply stricken. He's taking it to Chicago with him.

Jan said, That's nice for Kletkin, and opened the car door.

Madeline put her hand on Jan's wrist and lifted her hand. How's your hand, Jan? Victoria, did Jan tell you about the perfectly horrible thing that happened?

Victoria looked over Jan's arm. Why, yes, she said, looking up at Jan, but I, was it really bad?

Jan drew her hand away. She put the lobsters in the back of the car. What's so horrible about it? she said, looking at Madeline. I've cut myself dozens of times. It healed nicely and there'll barely be a scar.

Madeline slid across the seat. Well, it *was* horrible, she said. Get in, my dear. By the way, I saw you at the Mark the other night dancing with that divine-looking boy, what's his name?

Dan Warmun, Victoria said.

Yes, that's the one, Madeline said, fumbling with the keys. This mob makes me wild. She stared at the fish vendors and the crowds moving and she looked backward and shuddered and said, My God, what a jam! Automobiles were coming and going behind them, turning in and halting and backing and there was lots of noise and movement. Madeline leaned to look across Victoria. Jan, would you mind very much getting us out of here?

Of course, Jan said, getting out. She went around the front of the car. Madeline was wonderful. An ordinary woman couldn't possibly have thought of a thing like that so quickly. Victoria and Madeline moved over and she got in without looking at Madeline who put her arm along the back of the seat immediately and said, I shouldn't have parked down here at all. Comfortable, Victoria?

Oh, quite, Victoria said. There's lots of room.

Jan backed slowly and without difficulty into the

street and drove forward, falling into line and driving slowly. That wasn't bad, she said, looking at Madeline.

Madeline settled her arm around Jan's shoulders. But you're always so cold-blooded about traffic, Jan, she said. It makes me wild.

Jan laughed and Madeline's arm held her shoulders in a quick close nervous embrace. She was close and warm against Jan's right side. Cold blood is a convenience sometimes, Jan said, looking at the trunk on the car ahead. She leaned forward and looked at Victoria and smiled at her. Say something, Victoria.

Victoria smiled and Madeline moistened her lips and said, Victoria's meditating.

Of course, Jan said. Sorry, Victoria. Victoria smiled and looked at Jan's dark hand on the wheel and looked at her own hand. Jan, leaning forward and watching her, said, Do you really want to go this brawl at Ann's?

Victoria looked up quickly and Madeline said, Why certainly she does, Jan. And it isn't a brawl; they're all charming people and we're going to have supper. Jan has the maddest ideas about people, Victoria.

Jan crossed Taylor street and drew up. There you are, Madeline. She leaned forward and looked at Victoria and said, If you want to go we'll go, and she saw that Victoria wanted to go and she got out. You'll have no trouble now, she said, looking at Madeline and closing the door. She went around the front of the car and got in beside Victoria. If we're really going I ought to stop by and change, she said.

You're perfectly all right, Madeline said.

Jan smiled. But I haven't any shoes on and I sat in something black on the wharf and my pants are . . .

You know you never care in the least what you wear, Madeline said.

Of course, Jan said. But you and Victoria might.

She glanced at the speedometer which at that moment was quivering nervously at forty. You'd never know Madeline was timid about traffic, would you, Victoria?

THE room using various voices said, Well, there you are; did you get the lobsters? and, Oh, hello, Jan, and, Well, good heavens, what's got Jan out of seclusion? And Jan looked around and saw John Carr and Max and Olga and Barton and Tell and Robert and lots of people she didn't know but she didn't see Kletkin. She felt the quick sharp resentment for Madeline she thought was all over and finished and dead but Madeline with her hand on Victoria's arm was saying, Stand still, ladies and gentlemen, this is an introduction! Jan looked at Victoria and she was smiling the lovely shy smile and her face had the rose light and Jan knew this was exciting to her. Madeline said, Miss Victoria Connerly, and these people, reading from left to right, are, and just then Jan heard Kletkin laugh. She went to the doorway she knew opened into the library and looked into the room. Kletkin was sitting on John's desk like a stevedore on a bale of cotton and a little man with pink hair and a paler pink face was standing before him with his hands in the pockets of his jacket.

Jan said, Calling Mr. Kletkin, and went into the room.

Kletkin said, Well, I'll be damned! and smiled and got off the desk. He met her half way across the room and put his arm around her shoulders and smiled at Hergmeyer. Take a good look, he said. Know this one?

Hergmeyer took his hands out of his pockets. His face was a warm ripening apple. His eyebrows twitched and he clasped his hands and said, Why, most emphatically, yes! He smiled and bowed beautifully. Miss Jan Morale, he said.

Jan, Kletkin said, this is Hergmeyer.

Jan held out her hand. How do you do, Mr. Hergmeyer.

He held her hand tightly. I am delighted. He looked intently at her with his small bright eyes. I have been watching your work with the keenest interest, he said. I am indeed delighted. Jan drew her hand away and Hergmeyer looked at Kletkin and said, He has just told me that you have refused to have your name identified with this, this . . .

Go on, Kletkin said, laughing, say it.

. . . this magnificent piece he is completing, Hergmeyer said.

But my name has nothing to do with it, Jan said, smiling. I've done an old fisherman I know any number of times but I've never given *him* credit.

That is a different matter, Hergmeyer said. He was getting excited. Kletkin had seen it and he wanted Jan to see it too. He stood smiling, his arm around her shoulders. When Hergmeyer got excited he was a sight. This, Hergmeyer said, is a matter so entirely different, I am tem—

Sorry, Madeline said from the doorway, but Mr. Southwick's leaving and he's asking for you, Mr. Hergmeyer, and you, she smiled at Kletkin. You know his train leaves at six. She stood smiling and beautiful in the doorway and waited.

Kletkin dropped his arm and said, That's right, and Hergmeyer compressed his lips and then bowed to Madeline and said, Thank you. Kletkin said, See you in a minute, Jan, and Hergmeyer bowed again and they went past Madeline who smiled and looked at them with her eyes bright and dark. She came quickly to Jan and said, Darling, let's go out on the balcony. She opened one of the doors behind the desk and went out and leaned on the railing facing Jan.

Jan lit a cigarette and stood looking at her and

wondering if Victoria found it interesting in there with all those people. She was sure Victoria wouldn't do anything foolish about drinking but she said, Are there cocktails?

Madeline nodded. But you don't like them. Come out here, darling, and then I'll get you some of John's marvelous brandy. She was looking at Jan and holding herself quiet against the railing. Just for a moment, she said. I've got to talk to you.

Jan smiled. You *are* good at it, Madeline.

What? Madeline said.

Puppeteering, Jan said. You dance people around so nicely.

Madeline looked at her. No one dances you around, she said.

Jan went to the desk and put her leg across the corner and put ashes into John's big soapstone ashtray. She looked at the cuff of her trousers white against her brown ankle and the ties of her alpargata blue and she wondered if Victoria really found it interesting. She looked up at Madeline and began to swing her foot. Cat and mouse and the same old trap, she said, smiling.

Madeline gave it up suddenly and came back into the room. She came around the desk and stood close to it against Jan's leg and put her hands on Jan's arms. I could scream, she said very low, I could . . .

I, Jan said, could drop you off the balcony and go home happy but I'm not going to and you're not going to scream.

Madeline moistened her lips. Darling, why do you have to be so mean about it? She held herself close along Jan's leg and moved her body slightly rhythmically and Jan stood up pushing her away and saying, It's no good, Madeline. How many times do you want me to tell you?

Madeline stood looking at her and breathing rapidly.

I almost hit you then, Jan said. It would have been nice, wouldn't it? She walked away from Madeline and went out to look for Victoria but Victoria was sitting at the piano with Robert. Robert was playing Weiner Blut and Victoria looked happy about it. Jan looked around and felt her head growing cooler and saw Barton looking at her. He said, Come here, Jan. He was standing with Kletkin and Hergmeyer and John in front of the fireplace. Jan, Barton said, you've seen this thing of Kletkin's, what do you think about it? Is it good?

She put her thumb through one of Kletkin's belt-loops and looked at Hergmeyer and said, Mr. Hergmeyer gets paid for saying things like that; why don't you take his word for it?

Hergmeyer nodded, looking at her with his small bright blue eyes amused and grateful. Precisely! John and Barton laughed and Hergmeyer said, Precisely! I can assure you it is the finest thing he has ever done and as anyone knows that is saying a great deal, no?

No, Kletkin said, smiling. He took Jan's arm and said, Just a minute, to Hergmeyer. To Jan he said, This isn't a train and you're not Southwick but it's more important.

Now don't run off, John said. Ann or somebody's getting supper or tea or luncheon or something.

Don't worry, Kletkin said. Jan took her thumb out of his beltloop and went with him to a sofa beyond the fireplace. Sit down, he said, drawing her down beside him. This thing sits like a cloud, doesn't it? Listen, he said suddenly, now what about Colorado?

From the sofa Jan looked directly across the room at Victoria. She was picking out a tune with one hand for Robert. Tell was leaning on the piano laughing at her and Robert was smiling and Victoria was smiling too and very earnest. Jan said, I can't go, Kletkin, and watched Victoria being happy.

Kletkin said, You can. Inga's coming down from Seattle to go with us. Inga's my niece. She dances.

We all dance, Jan said, watching Victoria.

Kletkin looked at her. Been drinking?

Not a drop all day, Jan said. I mean we all dance for somebody. Tell for instance dances for Robert. Sparrow for you. John for Ann. She glanced up at a tall dark woman who said, Hello, Jan Morale. She couldn't remember the woman's name but she said, Hello.

Kletkin said, Hello, Marie, this's private.

Marie went on laughing rich laughter. I had an idea it was, she said.

Victoria was rising. She saw Jan and smiled at her and Jan rose. I wondered where you were, Victoria said, coming to the sofa.

Miss Connerly, Jan said, Mr. Kletkin.

Kletkin looked up at Victoria. Hello, he said without moving.

Victoria said, How do you do, and wondered if this big young old man could really be Kletkin the sculptor.

Jan said, Do you want to stay, Victoria? If you do, Kletkin will bring you home when you're ready, won't you, Kletkin?

Kletkin looked at her. Sure, he said.

Victoria looked at Jan. Are you going? Jan nodded and Victoria said, Then of course I shall go too.

Not if you'd rather stay, Jan said. Kletkin will take care of you, won't you, Kletkin?

Kletkin looked at her. Sure, he said.

So you see? Jan said, if you'd rather stay you . . .

Not leaving? Madeline said, slipping her arm around Victoria's waist and her other arm through Jan's arm.

Yes, Victoria said. You see, I have to go over home tonight and it's getting rather late.

Kletkin was sitting with his arms folded and his eyes going across and back and across the three faces. The girl was young and pretty and fresh as spring water and her voice sang like a brook running. Madeline was a cat. Jan looked blacker than usual.

If you have to go to the boat, Madeline said, you must let me drive you down. At the rate Ann's going now supper's hours away.

Kletkin took a big breath and stood up. He hated cat fights. It wouldn't occur to any of you to give her a hand, I suppose, he said, looking at Madeline.

Madeline laughed. But, my dear, she's got Carlo and I've already been shoved out three times. Ann and somebody are having a glorious argument right now about lobsters. What can I do about it?

Kletkin said, I'll see what *I* can do. To Jan he said, I want to see you tomorrow afternoon. He nodded to Victoria and left them.

Kletkin's a beast, Madeline said. Well, my dear, shall we say good-bye to John? She glanced at Jan and said, Jan never says good-bye to people, so come along. She took Victoria's arm and they went off and Jan went out into the hall and down into the entry and outside. She stood with her hands in her pockets, looking at the twilight and wondering when it was going to be all over and finished. There was music cascading down the hill from some house farther up and there was a moment of fine deep laughter and voices passing in the street below. Downtown there were lights spreading out and farther away on the hills there were small twinkling lights like stars through mist. Jan looked at the twilight and wished it were all over and finished.

TURNING into Market street Madeline leaned forward to look across Victoria. Jan, let's take Victoria over to Berkeley, shall we?

Oh, thanks, Victoria said, but I couldn't think of letting you.

I think it would be fun, Madeline said. I may not go back to Ann's at all. Shall we, Jan?

I couldn't think of letting you, Victoria said.

Jan said nothing. It wasn't the same; something had changed it and made it dismal and monotonous as slow rain. She got out and went with Victoria as far as the wicket. Five minutes, she said, looking at her watch.

Victoria looked at her. You weren't happy about this evening, were you, Jan?

No, Jan said. Were you?

I was until I saw you weren't, Victoria said.

Jan smiled a little. Next weekend we'll go out of town. Will you, Victoria?

Oh, yes, Victoria said. She was looking at Jan all the time and trying to find Jan. I'm sorry about this evening, she said earnestly.

I'm sorry too, Jan said.

The door rolled back behind them and suddenly hundreds of bodies, hundreds of feet began the slow sliding sound, the feet moving slowly, the bodies packed too tightly for natural movement, the great press of bodies moving toward the doorway.

Good-bye, Victoria, Jan said.

Jan, shall we have lunch tomorrow? Or tea or dinner?

Jan shook her head. The next day at dinner? I'll meet you.

Victoria looked at her and nodded and then passed the machine and added herself to the fringe of the crowd moving slowly toward the doorway and through it. Jan waited. After a moment Victoria turned and smiled and

Jan smiled. It was all right then.

Madeline was walking back and forth under the arcade. She put her hand through Jan's arm. Don't look so black about it, darling. Wasn't I nice to her?

Come on, Jan said.

But I *was* nice to her, Madeline said. You don't understand at all, darling. I'm really fond of her. She's terribly sweet. I don't blame you in the least, Jan, but why do you have to be so mean about it? If you'd be nice to me I wouldn't be silly at all, darling.

Jan opened the car door and said, Get in, I'll drive.

If you like, Madeline said.

I want to go home, Jan said. She went around the car and got in.

All right, Madeline said. She gave Jan the keys and tucked herself down beside her. Couldn't we take a little drive first, darling?

No, thanks, Jan said.

Madeline tucked herself closer. Jan thought how wonderful it would be to be starting off somewhere with Victoria, Victoria who loved to drive at night, Victoria with her hair whipping up in lovely curling wisps. She looked up and saw the stars scattered and clear in the early dark and Madeline said, Darling, please don't look so black about it. I'm not going to be silly. She lifted her head and said gently, Jan, does she really mean so much to you?

Yes, Jan said. She turned into Post street and wanted to be standing with Victoria in Post street and fog over the street and lights and people hurrying past.

You never were that way about me, Madeline said. This is something you think you can't do without and you knew all the time you could do without me very nicely, didn't you?

Jan looked at her. What do you want to say?

Madeline looked up and said, I love you so terribly. You don't seem to think of that at all. Am I just to snap my fingers and say, There it's over? You don't think of me at all. Jan, remember the time at Highlands? Jan glanced at her and she said, I wish we could drive down there tonight and do that again. I mean everything, just as it was that time.

Are you crazy? Jan said.

I'd love to be if you'd be too, Madeline said. Jan, that morning in the park when I saw you with her I wanted to kill her and then I wanted to die, Jan, and then I wanted to hurt you terribly. I don't mean with the scorper or whatever it was but . . .

I know, Jan said. Let's not talk about it.

No, what I mean is I don't mind your being in love with her, she's so terribly sweet, but, darling, why couldn't you . . .

Are you crazy? Jan said.

When you changed that way almost overnight, darling, Madeline said, you can't really blame me, can you?

Jan drew in along the curb and slipped the motor out of gear but didn't cut off the ignition. Sit up, Madeline. Look at me. You knew damned well it was all over months ago, didn't you?

I knew you thought it was, Madeline said, but you've never treated me nicely for more than a day at a time and, oh, darling, it's so silly. She took Jan's hand and held it between her hands and said, Darling, if you'll let me come tonight I'll promise you anything. I'll give you my word.

Without any warning Jan felt the dark swift pain and it darkened her face and she knew it was there still. She hated it and knew it was there and it sickened her. Madeline felt it in her hand and she said, I'll give you my word, darling.

Jan stared at the back of Madeline's hand covering her hand. You haven't any word, she said, but she knew it was there in her and it sickened her, but it was there.

Madeline locked the car and took the keys. Jan stared at her hand black against Madeline's hand. Come on, darling, Madeline said, and she opened the door and got out and Jan got out and Madeline drew her hand up under her arm and they went up the steps and Jan opened the street door and they went inside. Going up the stairs she knew it couldn't be true that they were going up the stairs like this together again. But she knew they were going up the stairs. She was terribly aware of Madeline and she hated it and it was sickening but it was true. Then why didn't she stop, why didn't she stop Madeline? Her throat was small and tender, why didn't she kill her? If she killed Madeline it would be all over and finished. Why didn't she? Because it was in her and deep, it had been acting sleep but it was there and hating it didn't matter. She unlocked the door. In the dark room she stood with her back against the door and something was dying in the room, something was dead.

THEY were awake and still in the morning light and when Madeline could see Jan's face clearly she said, Darling, please don't look so black and lost, wasn't I nice? You were darling. She pushed back Jan's hair and kissed her forehead and closed her eyelids with her lips and kissed them and kissed the hollows that seemed deeper under her cheekbones and said, Darling, I know what you think, but it's not true. I give you my word. She looked closely at Jan's thin dark face, searching for some sign, but there was none. The eyes were still and the gray deeper and darker, but there was nothing there. She put her lips in the cup at the base of Jan's throat and tasted salt and said, Darling, please don't look so lost about it. She looked closely at Jan's face and she knew suddenly and finally that this blankness was the invulnerability of absolute indifference and she said, Oh, darling, I can't believe it means so much to you.

She gave this moment, this knowledge a few tears. Jan gave it nothing.

OKAY, Kletkin said. You can go if you want to.

Jan drew her breath slowly and lit a cigarette and smoked half of it, standing in a quiet sleep by the window. Finally she looked at Kletkin and he was sitting on the bench with his big forearms hanging between his knees and his face young and beautiful with wonder. She supposed she ought to look at it now. She looked at it and thrilled like a kite in the wind and forgot everything. After a long while she moved toward it and said slowly, There's nothing like that in me, Kletkin, but it's a damned beautiful lie.

Kletkin looked up. A damned lie? he said.

I mean it's a lie but a damned beautiful one, Jan said. It seemed strange and wonderful to see herself there in cold inflexible bronze, it seemed right. But there's nothing like that in me, she said. There was wonder in the forehead and eyes and there was a small smile on the mouth, the lips thin and rather cruel but for the softness of the smile. The back and the backs of the thighs and calves had the surface warmth, the skin smoothness Kletkin always got on bronze and underneath this his wonderful strength. It seemed unbelievably strange and wonderful to her.

Kletkin looked at her and said gently, It's all right, isn't it? and she nodded and he smiled and said, Come here and I'll tell you something. She sat down beside

him and he put his hand on her knee and held his palm
there with his fingers stiffened. You look like hell today,
he said. If you'd cut it out and stop being a fool you'd
be able to see just how much of you there is in it. He
hit her knee softly with his flattened palm. I thought
you decided to put the harness on again. She sat looking
at herself with no breasts and a look of wonder in her
bronze eyes and Kletkin said, It gets you, doesn't it?
Jan, remember when you used to work like a mule driver
all day and read half the night and then say, Come on
let's take a walk before we turn in? He hit her knee with
his palm flattened. If I'd known then you were going
stale and soft on me like this I wouldn't have wasted
a min—

You haven't, Kletkin.

He looked at her. What you need, he said, is Colorado.

She smiled at the bronze face. I suppose I do, she
said, but I can't do it.

You can't do it, Kletkin said with the gentleness out
of his voice and the harshness there again. Sometimes
he wanted to shake hell out of her. Well, what in God's
name *can* you do?

I'll show you some time, she said. And in the mean-
time don't *you* get nasty.

Kletkin leaned back against the wall and folded his
arms. The gentleness was in his heart again and in his
voice and he said, Well, you come in here looking like
hell and ready to eat people's heads off, what's a guy
to say?

It's all right, Jan said, don't worry about it, Kletkin.

DOCTORS should prescribe trees, Jan said, taken through
the eyes of course and preferably with Victoria, supine
position, hands under the head.

Victoria smiled. They're wonderful, she said.

Do we have to go, Victoria?

Victoria put her hands over her eyes with the palms up. She lay quite still. Oh, Jan, if I dared, she said, with her fingers covering her eyes, if only I dared. It's been so heavenly beyond words, Jan, all of it every moment. She held her hands over her eyes and in the small voice with the shyness Jan loved she said, It's all gone now, isn't it, Jan?

Yes, Jan said.

I'm so glad. Victoria took her hands away from her eyes. Look at me, Jan. Jan turned her head and Victoria said, Jan, I'm so glad being here with me has taken it all away.

Jan smiled. You don't know how lovely you are, she said.

Victoria looked up into the trees again. It's been so heavenly, Jan. Oh, I hate to think it's almost over, it's been so heavenly beyond words. She pulled her bare knees up and looked up into the trees and said, Jan, dear, let's never grieve about things. Grieving is too silly.

Of course, Jan said, smiling a little.

I read a poem once, Victoria said, looking up into the trees, it's just twelve words long but it's a complete thing. It goes like this, Poor little leaves, we too are drifting, someday it will be autumn.

Oh, Victoria, Jan said. She stretched out her hand and took Victoria's hand and held it tightly.

They lay under the trees until there was no sunlight through the branches and then they went down the bank and dived together and swam slowly the length of the pool and came up onto the float together. The water seemed very warm now, the air cool. They sat on the float swinging their feet. Already the lamps were lit on the terrace and the reflection of the inn and the small rose lights lay clear on the water. They went up presently and dressed and then they went down to dinner on the terrace. There were stars over the trees now and Philippe their waiter was a moth drawn back to their light again and again. They made the last dinner last a long time. After dinner they sat smoking and looking at the pool and the dark trees, looking sometimes at each other and thinking, We must never lose this. Finally they went upstairs again and they packed and they were ready to go. Jan turned out the light and put her arms around Victoria and said, We must never lose this, we must never never lose this. It was a small room high in the slope of the roof and there were white geraniums growing in a box outside the window.

JAN stood behind Kletkin while he locked the door. She was very lonely standing behind Kletkin in the gray morning. A foghorn was bellowing itself hoarse.

Kletkin said, There! and straightened and turned around. He looked at Jan for a long time and then he put his hands on her shoulders and gripped them tightly. You're a wonderful fellow, he said, don't forget it. How's it going to be?

You know damned well how it's going to be, Jan said.

His big teeth showed. You're a wonderful fellow but you're crazy. Don't forget that either.

I won't, she said.

Stop looking like a hearse, he said, feeling like one. He put the key in his pocket and they went down the steps. Kletkin kept his arm around her shoulders. For two cents, he said, for a lot less than that I'd tap you behind the ear and throw you into the back of the car with the rest of the junk. Sparrow and Inga turned smiles upward. Kletkin said, So long, fellow, gripping her shoulders till they hurt and then went around the car and got in.

Jan gave her hands to Sparrow and Inga. Good-bye, she said, have a wonderful time. I'll keep an eye on David for you, Sparrow.

Oh, if you would, Sparrow said.

Inga said gravely, You should be coming too.

Inga was tall and splendid and out of Norse mythology. Jan smiled at her and at Sparrow, very little and brown beside Kletkin. Good-bye, Jan said. Have a wonderful time.

You said that, Kletkin said, smiling. And we hope you're bored to death.

Jan stood back from the running-board. She was very lonely, standing in the gray morning. The damned foghorn bellowed. She looked at Toothache beginning faintly to quiver. Kletkin's blue eyes and his mouth said, So long, fellow, and Toothache roared. Inga and Sparrow waved.

Good-bye, Jan said.

Kletkin backed into the street and turned around and headed down the hill. He leaned out to wave to her. She waved to him. She watched Toothache hide behind the hill. Toothache was a Packard born in 1924. Jan looked down into the fog and the damned foghorn bellowed like a strong man having big twin boys.

THE scar was a smooth pink line on her dark hand. She looked at it and felt nothing. She tried the spitzsticker on her nail. It was sharp. She did nothing about it. She sat looking at the scar on her hand. After a while she went into the alcove and got out two copper saucepans and scoured and polished them. She scoured and polished the coffeepot with less ferocity and with more care and some amusement. She went back then and picked up the spitz-sticker and it was good in her hand and she went to work. She worked slowly. Her work had a great leanness and simplicity, a pure and definite meaning. This was her reputation. She would never attempt the smallest detail until she was satisfied that her hands and her mind and her eyes had a perfect and harmonious awareness of their task. With this awareness she could work without pause and with no pattern on the block. She liked to work until fatigue came in a sudden thundering rush down into her back and arms and hands. She could rest quietly then; she could say to her heavy closing eyelids, Gently now, we're very tired.

SHE took David onto her arm and walked to the window with him. She stood looking out at five big golden pancakes steaming and melting butter on a sign-board. She nodded to them and said, Do you eat lots of pancakes for breakfast, David?

David smiled and kicked one foot and put his forefinger in her ear and bored.

She stood him on the window ledge and held him against the glass. Let me take a good look at you, she said. You *are* bigger, aren't you? And you're wearing socks. She picked him up and put him on her arm again. She looked at him and he smiled and found the lapels of her jacket and looked underneath them. Socks, she said. David, you've fallen from heaven, you're just a big softie. What about ice cream?

He kicked his foot vigorously and showed Jan his small white incisors. He forgot the lapels.

Jan went out into the hall with him. She heard Mrs. Cummings humming Stormy Weather in a room across the hall. Mrs Cummings, Jan said, looking at David, we're going to the drug store for ice cream. All right?

Oh, isn't that nice? Mrs. Cummings said. She came to the door and smiled and pouted at David and said, Now Davie, what do you say to Miss Morale?

David had nothing to say but he smiled and kicked his foot.

JAN, don't be angry. I had to come.

Angry, Jan said. Let me have the coat and things.

Victoria slipped out of her coat and took off her hat and her gloves and gave them to Jan. I'm sick about it, she said.

Here, Jan said, tossing a pillow onto the rug. Lie on the rug and tell me about it.

Victoria went slowly to the rug and sat down, hugging her knees and looking at the fire. Jan took off her smock and stretched out beside her. Victoria curled down onto the rug and put her face in the pillow. Jan put her arm around her and said, Tell me then.

Victoria lifted her head and put her hand over Jan's and said, Oh, it's so terrible I can't think about it. Jan, our lovely vacation's all over.

Over? Jan said.

It's gone, Victoria said. I've been counting the days till the fifteenth, and now it's gone.

Jan kissed her gently. Tell me.

Jan, last night dad came home almost bursting with something but he wouldn't tell us until after dinner and then he took mother's hand and said, My dear, how would you like to go to Chicago with Mary and Dan? Oh, Jan, if you could have seen them! You see that's where dad met mother, at that other Chicago exposition and mother's wanted so much to go to this one but of course she didn't dream of mentioning it to dad. But he planned it all with Mrs. Warmun and Dan so that he could get away when I had my vacation and Mrs. Warmun and Dan are going sooner so we all can be together. It's all planned and they're as happy as children about it, Jan.

Jan looked at her. Two swift summer weeks gone and nothing of them to be remembered. Well? she said.

I can't go, Jan, Victoria said, and I can't disappoint them. I can't go and I don't know how to tell them I can't. Mrs. Warmun and Dan came last night after dinner and they all sat there talking about it and saying, We'll go there, we'll go here, and, Jan, I wanted to die. If you could have seen mother and dad. Mother's been such an angel about everything, Jan, and this means so much to her. Jan, what can we do about it?

Jan looked at her. Do? Why, we'll eat more weekend crumbs.

Jan, I don't want to go, Victoria said. I won't go if you'll tell me what to do about it.

Do? Jan said. She felt buried in a long deep grave. They're fond of you, she said, looking at Victoria, they're devoted to you and you couldn't possibly disappoint them. What's to be done to a fact like that? Nothing. We couldn't possibly do a thing to it, my dear. It's a Gibraltar.

Jan, Victoria said, do you *want* me to go? I believe you really want me to go.

Jan shook her head. Don't say things like that. She brushed loose damp earth out of her eyes and stepped out of her grave. She kissed Victoria gently but with no feeling of gentleness. Damp earth has a bitter taste, she said. She looked at Victoria and smiled at her and said, It's one of those things you should have known, Victoria. There'll be things like this and you'll get used to them or you'll get tired of them; it'll depend on you.

I've got used to them. You see, my dear, you'll never be able to say to your family I'd rather go to the mountains with my friend than go to Chicago with you. You see that's simply a way of saying, My dear family, to hell with you, and you couldn't possibly be expected to say that.

Victoria put her hand over Jan's mouth. Oh, Jan, she said, Jan, don't!

Jan took her hand away and kissed it in the palm. Dear Victoria, she said. It's no good, is it? I'm sorry. She put her arms around Victoria and said, It's one of those things we can be sorry about but we can't grieve, you said so yourself. Now tell me what happened to you today. Did you get a run in your stocking? Tell me what you had at lunch. I had potato salad and two beautiful old herrings. Victoria, you should have seen them. I'll tell you. It seems that in their youth which of course they spent in the North Sea they were a sort of Damon and Pythias combination. But one day they were taken into different nets and subsequently packed into different barrels. Months passed and they wept for each other and flavored the barrels with their tears. But, Victoria, there really is some goodness in life. You see, one of them was packed into the top of a barrel, the other into the bottom of another barrel and these two barrels were shipped to Mr. Krauss down in Powell street and . . . Does biography bore you, Victoria?

Victoria moved her head and said no. She was smiling now and her eyes, her mouth were dreaming on Jan's face and she said, Oh, Jan, you're the loveliest person.

ONE card said, Hello, Jan. Made good time and everything OK. You're going to be poor all the rest of your life because you're missing this. Swimming better than swimming ever was. Inga like a trout in water and even better looking. Kletkin.

The next card said, Dear Jan, Kletkin grieves for you. Couldn't you come even yet? The lake is enchantment. The horses are magnificent. Inga.

The next card said, Dear Jan, How is it with you? Have you seen David? Sparrow's gained five pounds but she's going to lose it wondering if they've let D boil in the bath water. Please reassure her. I keep wondering if you've fallen on your sword. Then why don't you write? Kletkin.

The first letter came through the air and it said, Dear Jan, I cannot write this letter but I must. I cannot believe it has happened but it has. Kletkin was thrown yesterday and killed instantly. I cannot believe it. None of us can. I know how much he loved you. I know he put you above all people and believed in you always. It is so difficult to write this and I know it will be difficult for you to read and to comprehend and to bear. Forgive me for being unable at this time to write more fully.

Inga.

JAN was lying on the bed and Victoria moved quietly about; she opened windows and tried the door and then she went to the bed and lay down beside Jan. The moon was full and high and there were white screens of light at the windows. Victoria slipped her hand into Jan's and said, whispering, Jan, dear, if I could do anything, anything.

When Victoria was asleep Jan got out of bed and walked up and down the room with the barrenness.

MADELINE and Mrs. Keel looked up and looked startled

and Madeline said, Oh here she is now, and Mrs. Keel said, Oh, yes, here she is now. Jan looked at them and Mrs. Keel said, Good morning, and Madeline said, Hello, Jan. Jan said, Hello, and went past them and started upstairs. The stairs came down smoothly under her feet. She started at the touch on her arm and the stairs stopped moving.

Jan, Madeline said, Jan, do you hear me?

Of course, Jan said.

Madeline moistened her lips. She was shocked beyond expression, she had never seen Jan look like this. Jan, she said, I came to tell you how terribly sorry I am, I only just heard. She stared at Jan. She couldn't believe this was Jan.

Jan went on and the stairs came down smoothly under her feet. She was at her door before she noticed Madeline was beside her.

Jan, let me come in just for a moment, Madeline said. I'll make you a cup of coffee. Jan, you look terrible. You haven't eaten nor slept for days, have you?

She followed Jan in and closed the door. Jan pulled off her muffler and sat down in her coat and leaned her head back and closed her eyes. Madeline went to the alcove and put water to heat and sliced bread and made thin trimmed sandwiches. She made a pot of coffee and took a cup of it and the sandwiches over to Jan. The coffee'll pick you up, darling, and you ought to eat something, really. She put the tray on the table and leaned forward over Jan and kissed her and Jan opened her eyes. She saw Madeline's face close to hers and she woke out of a long terrible loneliness of sleep and she hated Madeline and this hatred was awake again and she rose swiftly striking Madeline's knees with hers, her body striking Madeline's like a tree falling in a storm. She caught Madeline's throat with her hands and she thought of nothing but the long humiliated hatred and her hands fitting Madeline's neck like a tight necklace. Madeline pushed out with her hands and that was futile and Jan smiled; she knew she was stronger and resistance was beautiful; it was a thing to prolong and subdue and finally kill and hold wilted in your hands. She knew Madeline with much white showing in her eyes was trying to say her name and she laughed. He was a beast, wasn't he? she said. Her teeth were locked tightly together and words came through them with a hissing sound. But you'll be where he is, she said, you'll be where he is, he'll show you. She slipped her thumb down to the base of Madeline's throat into the hollow she had kissed and Madeline struggled and clawed at her arms and it was all futile. This was the end of the weariness and the bitterness; it would make her loneliness a safe place. And then Madeline jerked backward, escaping the terrible numbing pressure of the thumb and gasped and said hoarsely, Jan, you're mad! and Jan's hands relaxed. She loosened her fingers and slid her hands out along Madeline's shoulders. She began to tremble and she held Madeline's shoulders tightly, hurting them in her hands but with no desire now to hurt. Madeline's head sagged forward between Jan's arms and she was crying in long broken gasps.

You're not hurt, Jan said. Once I was choked senseless and I came around and went to work on time. She held Madeline's shoulders tightly, trying to stop the dance of nerves all along her body and in her arms and hands. She watched Madeline lifting her head slowly out of a black sobbing terror.

Was he a beast? Jan said.

Madeline's head moved loosely left and right.

Jan nodded. And it's all over? It's finished?

Yes, Madeline said. She found her throat and

bandaged it with her hands and moaned softly. Jan, let me go.

You're not hurt, Jan said, looking at her. You're going to walk out of here and downstairs now and you're never coming back, are you?

No, Madeline said.

Jan breathed a deep breath and took her hands off Madeline's shoulders. She stood quite still and Madeline, released, hurried past her, almost running to the door.

SHE worked twenty hours a day for three days. On the fourth day she threw the disfigured blocks into the fireplace and drank a brandy and soda and wrote a letter to Sparrow and Inga. Dear friends, If he is dead I too am dead in a way you know. But you can't know. He was everything I had looked for in people and never found until I met him. He saved my life once. He fed me. He taught me all the good things I know. He was my father, my brother, he was the only friend I ever had. You can't know. I don't forget that he is lost to you too but I am not going to write about that now. You must let me know if there is anything I can do. When I saw David last he was happy and well. Jan.

IT'S our lake and our sky, even our little white sail but it's not the same, is it, Victoria?

Jan, Victoria said suddenly, I'm not going. I've made up my mind.

Jan looked at her and smiled a little. Dear Victoria, she said. You know you *are* going and you're going to have a wonderful time and you're not going to talk about it any more.

Jan, Victoria said, won't you go too? Because if you

won't I'm not going, not now.

Jan looked at the lake again and she was not seeing this lake but another lake she had never seen. It's already so far away, she said, I don't even remember how I felt about it at first. But nothing's changed, Victoria. I had a friend I'll never see again, that's all. Now I have only you. But nothing's changed. She smiled a little and said, If I hadn't met Kletkin I'd still be weighing paper in a dirty little print shop, I'd never have met you. She looked down at Victoria's hand with the jade ring holding the handlebar of her bicycle tightly. She touched Victoria's hand lightly and said, I'm sorry if I made you afraid, Victoria, but that's all over. Shall we go now?

Victoria said, All right, in a low voice and they wheeled their bicycles down the slope and mounted and rode on. It was a beautiful day, it was a day like another day. Victoria wearing sunglasses had no strangeness to Jan now.

JAN lay across the bed trying to read, trying to find something to read, turning the pages noisily and hunting. She smoked cigarettes quickly and got up twice and went to the window and looked down at the rain and at the dark shining tops of automobiles moving in the rain. But each time she went back to the newspaper on the bed and looked for something to read. Down in the street the newsboys were crying an extra. Little flies of anxiety buzzed and settled on her mind. She got up. Waiting had never been so long. The hotel slept with restless dreams of quick footsteps in corridors going nowhere.

The moment Victoria entered the room she began to cut Jan's hand to pieces with her nails. Oh, Jan, she said, Jan, it's so awful having to meet you like this and trying to make everything fit and I've kept you waiting so long.

Jan freed her hand and held Victoria's face and kissed the raindrops. It's not awful, she said, smiling, it's lovely. Lovely rain on the windows, lovely raindrops on your face, lovely Victoria breathless over nothing.

Oh, Jan, Victoria said, I can't bear it.

Let's take your coat off, Jan said. She unbuckled the belt and unbuttoned the coat and pulled the sleeves off Victoria's arms. She put the wet raincoat over the footboard of the bed and stood behind Victoria taking off her hat in the mirror. In the mirror Victoria had very large frightened eyes and damp darkened hair curling around her face. They looked at each other in the mirror.

Oh, Jan, Victoria said, turning.

They went to the bed and lay across it looking at each other and saying little unfinished things. Then Jan got up and turned out the light and lay on the bed with Victoria in her arms and rain and light on the windows and Victoria sweet and she said, You don't know how lovely you are, you don't know how much I love you.

Jan, Victoria said, I can't bear it.

Jan looked at the echo of these words. Victoria, she said, what if you never come back to me? What if . . .

Oh, Jan, Victoria said, don't!

Jan was silent for a moment and Victoria was silent and then Jan said, Did I tell you I have a commission, a very important one, to keep me busy? Oh, and I meant to tell you, Victoria, you'll go to the Institute of course and I want you to manage to go alone the first time. Will you do that, Victoria?

Victoria nodded her head yes. Her head was aching fearfully. Her heart was trying to ache. Jan, she said suddenly, we know it isn't just that I'm going away for two weeks, that doesn't matter, Jan, it's that I'm doing a weak thing; it's because I'm not strong enough to do the thing I really want to do.

Of course, Jan said gently. That's why you're going and that's why I'm afraid. I'm afraid of all the things we'll do because we're weak. You can't see the watch, Victoria, but I can and it's time for you to go. Say you're going to have a wonderful time. Tell me.

Yes, Victoria said.

That's an equivalent of I do, Jan said, it means nothing. Victoria, in a moment I'm going to turn on the light and we'll be two people in a room looking at each other and wondering why on earth they were afraid of the dark. I love you. I love you more than anything in the world and I want you to love me that way. Goodbye, Victoria.

THE rain streamed down the windows of the taxi and the meter ticked and ran away with itself like a watch when you're lying awake at night and can't sleep and your watch races and runs away with itself. Jan looked at her watch and held the taxi in front of the station for three minutes. Then she dismissed the taxi and entered the station. It had a great empty height like a cathedral but ugly and naked. Jan went quickly across it to the doors opening to the tracks. The train was panting like a big tired animal. Jan saw Victoria in a crowd and stopped. It seemed strange that Victoria should have so many friends. Jan looked at them curiously. Looking at them she felt the taste of damp earth in her mouth and she didn't know why. The man and the boy beside Victoria were of course her father and Dan. She looked at Victoria's father and he was smiling and saying amusing things to a lot of young people. She didn't look at Dan. Dan and

Jan. She hadn't thought of that before. It would be a simple thing to confuse the names on the tip of your tongue and say one when you meant the other. Victoria was smiling and looking very beautiful and looking at all the faces and beyond them, but she didn't see Jan.

At the last moment the men stood back and the girls swarmed around Victoria and kissed her carefully because of their mouths and hers and said, Good-bye, good-bye, good-bye! and Victoria smiled at them and at the porter and stepped up and waved and her eyes were looking everywhere. The train was moving. Jan stood with her hands in the pockets of her trench-coat and her fists pressed into her groins. The train was moving and Dan was with Victoria on the steps and their hands were waving and Victoria's eyes were looking everywhere, the train was moving and the shed was echoing with the sound of the train moving and the voices of the girls saying, Good-bye, good-bye!

A few of the publications of
THE NAIAD PRESS, INC.
P.O. Box 10543 • Tallahassee, Florida 32302
Mail orders welcome. Please include 15% postage.

We Too Are Drifting by Gale Wilhelm. A novel. 128 pp.
ISBN 0-930044-61-4 — $6.95

A Hot-Eyed Moderate by Jane Rule. Essays. 252 pp.
ISBN 0-930044-57-6 — $7.95
ISBN 0-930044-59-2 — $13.95

Inland Passage and Other Stories by Jane Rule. 288 pp.
ISBN 0-930044-56-8 — $7.95
ISBN 0-930044-58-4 — $13.95

Amateur City by Katherine V. Forrest. A mystery novel. 224 pp.
ISBN 0-930044-55-X — $7.95

The Sophie Horowitz Story by Sarah Schulman. A novel. 176 pp.
ISBN 0-930044-54-1 — $7.95

The Young in One Another's Arms by Jane Rule. A novel. 224 pp.
ISBN 0-930044-53-3 — $7.95

The Burnton Widows by Vicki P. McConnell. A mystery novel.
272 pp. ISBN 0-930044-52-5 — $7.95

Old Dyke Tales by Lee Lynch. Short Stories. 224 pp.
ISBN 0-930044-51-7 — $7.95

Daughters of a Coral Dawn by Katherine V. Forrest. Science
fiction. 240 pp. ISBN 0-930044-50-9 — $7.95

The Price of Salt by Claire Morgan. A novel. 288 pp.
ISBN 0-930044-49-5 — $7.95

Against the Season by Jane Rule. A novel. 224 pp.
ISBN 0-930044-48-7 — $7.95

Lovers in the Present Afternoon by Kathleen Fleming. A novel.
288 pp. ISBN 0-930044-46-0 — $8.50

Toothpick House by Lee Lynch. A novel. 264 pp.
ISBN 0-930044-45-2 — $7.95

Madame Aurora by Sarah Aldridge. A novel. 256 pp.
ISBN 0-930044-44-4 — $7.95

Curious Wine by Katherine V. Forrest. A novel. 176 pp.
ISBN 0-930044-43-6 — $7.50

Black Lesbian in White America. Short stories, essays,
autobiography. 144 pp. ISBN 0-930044-41-X — $7.50

Contract with the World by Jane Rule. A novel. 340 pp.
ISBN 0-930044-28-2 — $7.95

Yantras of Womanlove by Tee A. Corinne. Photographs.
64 pp. ISBN 0-930044-30-4 — $6.95

Mrs. Porter's Letter by Vicki P. McConnell. A mystery novel.
224 pp. ISBN 0-930044-29-0 — $6.95

To the Cleveland Station by Carol Anne Douglas. A novel.
192 pp. ISBN 0-930044-27-4 — $6.95

The Nesting Place by Sarah Aldridge. A novel. 224 pp.
ISBN 0-930044-26-6 — $6.95

This Is Not for You by Jane Rule. A novel. 284 pp.
ISBN 0-930044-25-8 — $7.95

Faultline by Sheila Ortiz Taylor. A novel. 140 pp.
ISBN 0-930044-24-X — $6.95

The Lesbian in Literature by Barbara Grier. 3d ed.
Foreword by Maida Tilchen. A comprehensive bibliography.
240 pp. ISBN 0-930044-23-1 — $7.95

Anna's Country by Elizabeth Lang. A novel. 208 pp.
ISBN 0-930044-19-3 — $6.95

Prism by Valerie Taylor. A novel. 158 pp.
ISBN 0-930044-18-5 — $6.95

Black Lesbians: An Annotated Bibliography compiled by
JR Roberts. Foreword by Barbara Smith. 112 pp.
ISBN 0-930044-21-5 — $5.95

The Marquise and the Novice by Victoria Ramstetter.
A novel. 108 pp. ISBN 0-930044-16-9 — $4.95

Labiaflowers by Tee A. Corinne. 40 pp.
ISBN 0-930044-20-7 — $3.95

Outlander by Jane Rule. Short stories, essays. 207 pp.
ISBN 0-930044-17-7 — $6.95

Sapphistry: The Book of Lesbian Sexuality by Pat Califia.
2nd edition, revised. 195 pp. ISBN 0-930044-47-9 — $7.95

The Black and White of It by Ann Allen Shockley.
Short stories. 112 pp. ISBN 0-930044-15-0 — $5.95

All True Lovers by Sarah Aldridge. A novel. 292 pp.
ISBN 0-930044-10-X — $6.95

A Woman Appeared to Me by Renee Vivien. Translated by
Jeannette H. Foster. A novel. xxxi, 65 pp.
ISBN 0-930044-06-1 — $5.00

Cytherea's Breath by Sarah Aldridge. A novel. 240 pp.
ISBN 0-930044-02-9 — $6.95

Tottie by Sarah Aldridge. A novel. 181 pp.
ISBN 0-930044-01-0 — $6.95

The Latecomer by Sarah Aldridge. A novel. 107 pp.
ISBN 0-930044-00-2 — $5.00

VOLUTE BOOKS

Journey to Fulfillment	by Valerie Taylor	$3.95
A World without Men	by Valerie Taylor	$3.95
Return to Lesbos	by Valerie Taylor	$3.95
Desert of the Heart	by Jane Rule	$3.95
Odd Girl Out	by Ann Bannon	$3.95
I Am a Woman	by Ann Bannon	$3.95
Women in the Shadows	by Ann Bannon	$3.95
Journey to a Woman	by Ann Bannon	$3.95
Beebo Brinker	by Ann Bannon	$3.95

These are just a few of the many Naiad Press titles. Please request a complete catalog!

LOOK FOR THESE BOOKS
TO BE PUBLISHED IN 1985

CHECK YOUR LOCAL BOOKSTORE
OR WRITE US ... BE SURE YOU
ARE ON OUR MAILING LIST!

Inland Passage and Other Stories by Jane Rule

A Hot-Eyed Moderate, Essays by Jane Rule

The Swashbuckler, A Novel by Lee Lynch

Sex Variant Women in Literature by Jeannette Howard Foster

Misfortune's Friend, A Novel by Sarah Aldridge

Lesbian Nuns by Rosemary Curb and Nancy Manahan

A Studio of One's Own by Ann Stokes, Edited by Dolores Klaich

An Emergence of Green, A Novel by Katherine V. Forrest

Torchlight to Valhalla, A Novel by Gale Wilhelm

Plus some surprises . . .

FROM

The Naiad Press, Inc.
P.O. Box 10543
Tallahassee, Florida 32302